Carlota. Riding her stallion at top speed, racing and beating the neighboring rancheros, and branding cattle, Carlota proves herself again and again; she is courageous and strong, surely the equal of all her dead brother Carlos could have been. In the conflict between Don Saturnino's need for a son and the outraged sense of a woman's place voiced by her proud grandmother, Carlota has always sided with her father. It is not until she rides out with the men to ambush Kit Carson and the Yankee army in what would be later known as the Battle of San Pasqual, not until she wounds a young soldier with her lance, that Carlota comes face to face with her own feelings of tenderness and compassion and defies her father in defining herself.

Set against the turbulent backdrop of the last days of the struggle between the Californians and the Americans, the Mexican War, this is the story of an unusual young woman and her final grasp of the complexity of true strength.

Also by
SCOTT O'DELL
The Black Pearl
Child of Fire
The Cruise of the Arctic Star
The Dark Canoe
The Hawk That Dare Not Hunt by Day
Island of the Blue Dolphins
Journey to Jericho
The King's Fifth
Sing Down the Moon
The Treasure of Topo-el-Bampo
The 290
Zia

Carlota

SCOTT O'DELL

1977

Houghton Mifflin Company Boston

Library of Congress Cataloging in Publication Data
O'Dell, Scott, 1903-
   Carlota.
   SUMMARY: A young girl relates her feelings and
experiences as a participant in the battle of San Pasqual
during the last days of the war between the Californians
and Americans.
   1. San Pasqual, Battle of, 1846 — Juvenile fiction.
[1. San Pasqual, Battle of, 1846 — Fiction. 2. California — History — To 1846 — Fiction] I. Title.
PZ7.0237Car [Fic] 77-9468
ISBN 0-395-25487-6

Author's Note

President Polk fervently believed that California,
and the rest of the Southwest, belonged to the
United States by right, by Manifest Destiny. He
was joined in this belief by a strong faction in
Congress who wanted to extend slavery from the
South into the West. Between them, they deliber-
ately provoked Mexico into attacking the United
States in the year 1846.

The war that followed was fought mostly in
Mexico and Texas. In California, which Mexico
had won from Spain only a few years before, the
ruling class, those who had come to California
from Spain, were divided in their loyalties. Some
wanted the United States to win. Some hated the
gringos and wanted Mexico to win. Others, and
they were in the majority, didn't much care who
won so long as they were left to follow their pas-
toral ways. In time, if left alone, they would have

v

revolted from Mexico and founded a republic of their own. Though they felt no love for the gringos, the de Zubaráns, for most of this story, belonged to the last group.

The war as it was fought in California was not a war but a series of comic-opera skirmishes. American adventurers, like General Frémont, marched up hills, raised flags, and marched down the hills again. There was one exception. After California had been overrun, a handful of Spanish lancers, out of pride and desperation, surprised and bloodily defeated General Kearny's Army of the West in the peaceful valley of San Pasqual.

The story of Carlota de Zubarán is based in part upon the life of Luisa Montero, who lived in southern California, near Mount Roubidoux, in the early years of the last century. Details of the San Pasqual battle are taken from the reminiscences of Juan Palomares and Kit Carson, and from the diary of Lieutenant Emory, a topographical engineer with General Kearny's Army of the West.

Trees and the tall grass bent. Clouds curled down from the mountains. Lightning forked through the sky, and thunder crashed. Wedges of rain slowly descended upon the Ranch of the Two Brothers.

My grandmother sat in her rocking chair and watched the storm beat against the windows. "It is a good sound the rain makes," she said. "I prefer it to the sound of bells or of birds, or of most anything."

Her cornhusks were in a tray on the table. She picked out one and took a double pinch of tobacco from a silver box. She sprinkled it into the husk and carefully rolled herself a long, thin cigarillo. Then she looked around for Rosario.

"Fire!" she shouted.

Young Rosario was in the courtyard, but he heard her screech and came running. He went to the fireplace and picked out a coal and quickly lit her cigarillo.

Doña Dolores settled back and began to puff and rock. She liked her chair because it fit her bony bottom. It had come from a place called

Boston, thousands of miles away. She had had it for just a week.

"The only thing wrong with this chair," my grandmother said, "is that it was made by a gringo. Things made by gringos always have something wrong with them. Offhand it is difficult to say what will go amiss. It may develop a creak, like the last one. Or an arm will come loose. Or a rocker will fall off and pitch me on the floor."

"This one looks stout," I said.

"It is hard to tell what will happen to anything bought from a Yankee trader. Do you remember the wooden nutmegs I bought from a gringo?"

"That was before I was born."

"So it was. But imagine, nutmegs made of wood. They looked precisely like real nutmegs. And a polite, handsome young man sold them to me."

Grandmother struck the floor with the tip of her cane. "And now that the gringos have won the war, matters will be even worse."

The war my grandmother spoke about was the war between America and Mexico. We, the *Californios*, those whose ancestors came from Spain, were drawn into the fighting against our will. We had few quarrels with America. Nor many ties with Mexico; and it irked us that we were ruled by despots who lived a thousand leagues away. We wished only to be left to ourselves, to spend our lives in peace. This, we had learned, could not be done.

"The gringos have not won the wars," I said. "Yesterday I heard that we had beaten them in a battle somewhere in the North."

"Somewhere. It is always somewhere. The *Californios* have not won a single battle since the war began. And how could they when there is not one man among us who wishes to fight? The weasel-livered young think only of dancing and cards. The old are tired and do not care who rules them so long as they are left alone. The war is lost. It was lost the day it began. There are thousands of gringos. Who cares?"

"I care and you care."

"Little difference that makes. Two women. What of the men? What of Don Saturnino?"

"He will fight to protect the ranch. He and all the vaqueros and our Indians."

"Talk. Talk. The war is lost. A horde of locusts waits to descend upon us."

Doña Dolores always looked upon the dark side. I didn't feel that the war was lost. Perhaps in the North, but not here in California del Sur. Not here, ever.

Grandmother rocked and puffed and watched the rain beating against the window. Presently she

3

finished the cigarillo and rolled another. Again she shouted for Rosario.

After he had come and lit her cigarillo, he got down on all fours in front of her and she put her feet on his back. I am sure he didn't like to be used as a footstool. Nor did I like it. He belonged to the tribe that had killed my brother, and this was the punishment my father had decreed. Rosario was ten years old, but he was no larger than a five-year-old; just a small bag of skin and bones, with small black eyes like copper centavos. What his Indian name was I do not know. He was a Piute Indian my father had captured in a raid when Rosario was only two.

"How long do you think the rain will last?" I said.

"Ten years ago, in the winter of thirty-six, it rained for a month. It almost washed the ranch away."

"The sky looked the way it does now, like a great gray blanket."

"*Exactamente*," Doña Dolores said. She gave me one of her sharp, bodkin looks. "Why are you so concerned about the rain?"

I had never lied to my grandmother, except once. Sometimes to my father and often to my sister. But never to my grandmother, because she had a good memory and usually found me out.

"There's a horse over at Jamal. He's a palomino, about two years old. I want to ride over and bring him back."

My grandmother blew smoke through her nose, two thin streams, and thought about something for a long while.

"This riding business," she said. "One of the vaqueros reports that he saw you riding Tiburón, the black stallion. Is that the truth?"

"It is true."

"With a leg on one side of the horse and a leg on the other side. Astride! Is that also true?"

"It is also true."

"Do you know that young ladies or ladies of any age do not ride stallions? That they ride mares and geldings, but not stallions?"

"I do."

"How long have you known this?"

"For ten years. Since I was six and you told me."

"When did you start with the stallion?"

"This summer, in June."

"And with the legs on each side?"

"Yes. Otherwise it is hard to ride. You do not stay on a stallion if both of your legs are dangling on one side."

"Is it necessary to ride a stallion?"

"No, but it is more fun than to ride a mare."

Doña Dolores's cigarillo had gone out and Rosario brought another coal from the fireplace.

"This business of the stallion is the fault of your father," my grandmother said. "He should not have encouraged you to ride the stallion with your legs helter-skelter."

This was true, what she said about Don Saturnino. He had put me on a horse when I was only six years old. He sat me in his silver-studded saddle and walked the horse around the corral. We walked for most of an hour while he told me things about a horse. When my first lesson was over, he said for me not to say anything to my grandmother about what we had done. I promised not to and I didn't. The next day she asked me about the riding. She had heard of it from a vaquero, Felipe, the same one who had just told her about the stallion. I acted as if I had never been near a horse. Although I did not tell a lie, the way I acted it was still a lie.

It was the only lie I ever told her, for the next morning, while I was riding around the corral and my father was walking beside me, she suddenly appeared. She was lame and walked with a stick, but there she was, a half-league almost from the house, peering at us between the rails of the fence. And there I was, astride.

"So this is what goes on under my very eyes,"

she said in her calmest voice. "A scandal."

"Dear Mother," Don Saturnino said. "One day my Carlota will be good on a horse if, if you leave us alone."

"She still does not need to ride like an Indian. In my youth I rode sidesaddle from here to Los Angeles, which is more than fifty leagues."

"How long did it take you, Doña Dolores? This ride to Los Angeles. How many weeks?"

"Not even one week. Six days and a half, to be correct."

"If you had ridden astride in the manner I teach Carlota, then you could have reached Los Angeles easily in half the time."

"And have the countryside talk about me as they will talk about my granddaughter? It is an embarrassment. It is a scandal. It is unsupportable." Sometimes my grandmother liked big words.

"Once Carlota rides a horse as it should be ridden," my father said, "and the countryside, as you call it — I presume you mean the Bandinis and the Palomareses — when these upstarts . . ."

The Bandinis and the Palomareses both had received their grants and moved from Mexico many years after we, the de Zubaráns, had settled upon Rancho de los Dos Hermanos. These were the people my father and his mother were talking about.

7

"When the upstarts see how beautifully she rides," my father went on, "how swiftly and how elegantly, they will copy her. All of their daughters will be riding astride within a year's time, as if they had always ridden that way. Indeed, as if they themselves, and they alone, had set the fashion."

"I do not care the flick of my little toe about either the Bandinis or the Palomareses," Grandmother replied. "I care about my own sense of what is proper."

Doña Dolores had paused to dab at her nose, as she stood there at the corral when I was only six years old.

Sometimes when she saw that she wasn't about to get her way, my grandmother dabbed at her eyes with a dainty pink handkerchief she always carried in her sleeve. But this morning she didn't use it. Instead, she went clumping off, swinging her stick back and forth as if warding off a horde of enemies.

"She is very angry," my father said. "We had best not ride for a week or so until she simmers down."

This did not please me, but I was then an obedient daughter, as I am now, mostly, and said nothing.

While the rain increased and beat loud upon the

roof, my grandmother fell quiet. For a while I thought she was asleep. But suddenly she reached out and with the toe of her fine vicuña shoe gave Rosario a dig in the ribs.

"Off with you," she said, "and see that Anita brings my chocolate. We have nine servants, three cooks, two ironsmiths, two carpenters, two harness-makers, four weavers, one *mayordomo,* and twelve vaqueros. Yet with all this army, nothing is ever done."

"There are too many captains in the army," I said, easing myself toward the door. I did not get there.

"Before you leave," Doña Dolores said, "let us talk more about the business of the stallion."

She paused and examined me from the tip of my boots to the red bandana that bound my hair.

"Once you looked like a girl," she said. "That was before you started riding around the country like an Indian. Your legs were always too long, but now they have stretched out. Your skin is the color of horsehide that has been cured for a year. And your hair has long sun streaks in it. The only thing about you that looks like a girl are your eyes, the golden eyes of the de Zubaráns, for which you can take no credit and which, no matter what you do, can you ever change. And the white teeth, also."

Rosario came back and got down on his hands and knees and my grandmother very delicately put her tiny feet upon his back. She fixed me with her steady gaze. Behind it I could see her mind working.

← · 2 · →

The rain was coming down. It was running off the roof in a waterfall and down the trail that led to Los Angeles and down the trail to San Diego. It was running everywhere.

"The way the rain looks now," my grandmother said, "it may last for a week. Perhaps two weeks. It is coming from the sea. From the sea the rain has much endurance."

My grandmother took her eyes off me and began to rock slowly. Then she rocked faster and looked out the window for a while.

"If the rain falls for two weeks," she said, "creek beds dry for years will swell. Rocks as big as houses will block the trails; the Los Angeles river that you can jump without wetting a shoe will run from bank to bank. The Santa Ana on its way to the sea will take forests with it. Then we can postpone the thing until spring comes. God, Who is on my side, can do much by spring."

The "thing" my grandmother referred to was the wedding of my sister, Yris, to Don Roberto Peralta.

11

"Perhaps He can think of something bigger than a flood," Doña Dolores went on. "Like an earthquake, where the countryside opens and scares the wits out of everyone. The last time the earth opened up was nine years ago. It is time for another, like the one that shook all of Helena Yorba's china out of her cupboard. The set she bought from a Yankee trader, and bragged that she had paid one hundred cows for, fell right out on the floor and broke into a thousand small pieces."

"Perhaps Don Roberto will change his mind," I said. "He has changed it before."

"He has no mind to change," my grandmother replied. "Don Roberto is a worm. But it is not his fault. His father is also a worm. Roberto has been told that it is for the de Zubaráns and the Peraltas to join in marriage. Two of the great families of California to be made one. Don Roberto believes what he is told."

"It may be a good marriage," I said, though I didn't think so.

"If the marriage will be so good," my grandmother quickly answered, "why did you not think of marrying Don Roberto yourself? It is you who are the older. Yris is two years younger than you. Who in this life ever heard of a younger sister marrying first? It is wrong. It is never done. It is likewise a scandal."

Rosario started to sneeze and Doña Dolores lifted her feet until he had sneezed three times and stopped.

"Do you wish to do your grandmother a great service?" Doña Dolores said.

"Yes," I said without warmth. "I wish to."

"Wishes are very cheap. *Muy barato.* Will you?"

"What is it that you wish?"

"I wish for you to marry Don Roberto."

I thought my grandmother was going to ask me to give up my stallion. I was not ready for an answer about Don Roberto.

"I will think about it," I said to gain time.

"Good," said my grandmother. "Begin to think about it now, at this moment."

She gave Rosario a prod with her foot.

"Go fetch my son," she said. "Whatever he is doing, fetch him."

Rosario scuttled off and my grandmother and I looked at each other warily and said nothing until my father came.

Don Saturnino was not tall, not so tall as I am, but he was stout-chested. He had small narrow feet and he was very proud of them. In a big chest he had sixteen pairs of boots, all beautifully stitched, of the best leather, and, to suit the way he felt, of many colors.

He bowed to his mother, taking off his sombrero and clicking his heels.

"It rains," he said.

"To good purpose," Grandmother said.

"What is the purpose? We do not require floods and torrents."

"The marriage," Doña Dolores answered. "It gives time to make changes. Roberto can marry Carlota instead of Yris."

"Don César and I have thought of the marriage. We have talked about it for five years."

"It is not proper that the younger daughter marry first."

"Don César and I have given thought to everything. This as well. It is not what is proper, but what is best for Yris and Carlota."

My grandmother puffed away calmly. She shifted her feet, looking for Rosario's back, but Rosario had not returned. He was outside, under the *portale*, feeding the big eagle that belonged to my father.

"Carlota and Don Roberto," Father said scornfully, pulling at his pointed beard. "Have you asked their permission?"

"Permission," Doña Dolores replied, "as you well know, is not required."

"It would be prudent, nonetheless," Don Satur-

14

nino said, keeping his temper. "Carlota is not Yris. She is a true de Zubarán."

"The difference is great," my grandmother said. "This I admit. You have seen to that. You have raised Carlota as a vaquero. She thinks of nothing but horses. Gray horses. Bay horses. White horses. Spotted horses. Palominos. Horses! She will not walk fifty steps. Instead, she will get on a horse and ride the distance."

What she said was true. I *had* been raised as a vaquero. I had been taught to do everything a horseman could do. My father had even named me after his son, Carlos, who had ben killed by the Piutes.

"Yris is a girl of the *sala,* good at needlework and the viola," Doña Dolores said. "She is not suited to Don Roberto."

"Neither is Carlota," my father said. "Nobody is suited to Don Roberto. That he is Don César's only son is a misfortune."

"The hairy worm," my grandmother said. "It is your fault. You might have found one of the Bandinis for her. Or even a Yorba. All else failing, one of the numerous Palomareses."

Doña Dolores bounced up from the chair and hobbled to the window and gazed out at the rain falling. I saw her cross herself and I knew that she

15

was praying for the rain to last forever. I walked to the door, leaving them to continue their talk, which would grow very fierce before it ended.

It did not trouble me. I had no intention of marrying Don Roberto, with his fat cheeks and fat little hands. And whatever Doña Dolores threatened — she sometimes said during these fights that she, and she alone, was the owner of the forty-seven-thousand-acre Rancho de los Dos Hermanos — but whatever she threatened, my father would never consent to such a marriage.

Furthermore, he would try to keep me at his side, as long as ever he could. And I did not mind the thought. I liked to ride with the vaqueros. I liked to go with my father and do the things he did. The truth was, as my grandmother often said, I thought little of anything except horses, all kinds and colors of horses. Nothing pleased me more than to be in my cordovan saddle with the big silver spurs on my heels.

~ · 3 · ~

After five days the rain ceased. The sun came up
in a bright cloudless sky as I began my weekly
inspection of our buildings. I did not care very
much for this task, but it had to be done and my
father wanted me to do it. I had been doing it
now for more than a year.

The ranch house was built of adobe, which is
mud mixed with straw and made into big bricks
and set out in the sun to dry. The walls of the
house were very thick, almost as thick through as
the reach of my outstretched hands. There were
few windows, only two on each side of the house,
and these were iron-barred and shuttered.

The house was built in the shape of a hollow
square. Each side was ninety long strides in
length. The roof, which was made of tile, was
proof against the flaming arrows the Indians liked
to use whenever they raided us. The house was a
stronghold, like the fortresses in Spain.

I always started at the big gate. There was a
small garden on one side of the gate and here my
father kept his pet eagle. It was Rosario's duty,

when he wasn't running errands or serving as a footstool for my grandmother, to tend the eagle. The bird's name was Vuelo Grande, which means Big Wing.

Old man Tiburcio, who had been a vaquero but now was too old to work the cattle, gathered mice and gophers to feed the bird. He caught them in traps every day and put them in a wicker cage and early in the morning set them inside the big gate where the eagle sat.

Vuelo Grande was screaming for his breakfast. He sat on his perch with a silver-link chain around one leg, flapping his wings and turning his neck first one way then the other, even backward like an owl. His eyes were large and hooded. They were green, with some yellow and brown spots in them. His eyes never seemed to look at you. They looked through you at something far away in the hills, in the mountains, beyond the mountains.

Rosario came running from somewhere and picked up the wicker cage. He reached in and took out a gopher, with care because it had long, sharp teeth.

"*Hola!*" he shouted to the eagle. "Catch!"

With one claw Vuelo Grande caught the gopher in mid-air.

"You have taught him a new trick," I said.

"Yes. And soon," Rosario said, "he will permit me to stroke his feathers."

"The feathers are very pretty," I said, "but take care that he doesn't get the claws in you."

"He is a brother," Rosario said. "He is an Indian bird."

"True. He comes from the Piute country. But remember that perhaps he doesn't know that you are brothers."

"He knows," Rosario said, and got ready to toss him a second gopher.

Next I visited the forge, where two young men were beating out shoes for the riding horses. Four that they had made especially for Tiburón hung on a peg. Next door was the saddlery. Here they made braided riatas and silver-studded saddles for the family and common saddles for the vaqueros. The weaving room was next. I did not go in. Through the open door I could see piles of yellow wool, still oily after the shearing. The looms were clicking and the spindles hummed. The Indian girls who tended them were in a happy mood now that they were no longer required to work on Sundays. It had been my idea to give them one day of rest. Doña Dolores opposed it, but with my father's help, I had won out.

I went quickly past the family rooms for fear that my grandmother might see me and call me in to do something for her. She had three servants, counting Rosario, and I didn't like to be used as a fourth one. I crossed myself as I passed the chapel, where I had already prayed at dawn.

My father sat in the sun beneath the *portale*. He sat here every morning when the sun shone and had his first cup of chocolate.

"*Qué pasa?*" he said. "Everything is in bad condition as usual?"

"In good condition," I said.

"How's the grandmother this morning?"

"I have not seen her."

"That is fortunate. You start the day well."

Don Saturnino sat on a three-legged stool, his legs spread wide, his long black hair hanging down his back. It glistened like the tail of a horse.

Hovering over him was Alfonso, the barber, combing his hair with a heavy horse comb. When that was done the barber braided it carefully and piled it on top of Don Saturnino's head and anchored it there with stout iron pins.

His hair combed and braided and bound in a flashy red handkerchief with yellow tassels hanging down his back, my father strode into the kitchen, where he ate his first meal of the day. I followed him and, as was proper, waited until he asked me to sit down.

The food came on in a flood. Pinto beans

cooked with *chile verde* and slivers of fresh beef, sprinkled with strong goat cheese. Tortillas as thin as the knife blade in my father's garter. Thick chocolate, beaten to a bubbly froth, a haunch of venison. *Tripes de leche* from a yearling cow. A pot of quail. Did the King of Spain eat better, I wondered.

My father said nothing to me until he had finished his breakfast and gone out into the courtyard for a glance at the weather.

Off to the west there was a small cloud. The wind blew gently from the south.

"Tomorrow," he said, "will also be fair."

"You're always right about the weather," I said.

"Wrong about much but not of the weather?"

"I did not say that."

"You did not so much as think it?"

"No, Father. Not a thought."

"What thoughts do you have about the wedding?" he said. "With fair weather coming, what day would you choose if it were your wedding?"

My father often asked my advice about things, then did what he wished.

"In two weeks is the day of Saint James. How does that suit?"

"As well as any day," said Don Saturnino. "Do we have sufficient paper for the invitations?"

"A sackful."

"Where?"

"It is in Doña Dolores's keeping."

"Go then and tell her to begin. Take five candles of deer tallow and a handful of goose quills and a jug of ink."

"Yes, señor."

"Who comes to the wedding?"

"A hundred, I fear. Maybe two hundred. Perhaps twice that many."

"Ayee!" my father cried. "We will have to go to the well."

The well my father spoke of was not a well at all, as I will explain. The past year had been a year of good grass but poor prices. The best of hides brought only twenty centavos. Except for the well, the ranch would have suffered.

"We will go and dip out a bucket of water," said my father. "We will go soon. We will go tomorrow."

"*Vámanos*," I said. "Let us go."

◄ · 4 · ►

My father wore the heaviest of his leather breeches, his thickest jacket, and a pair of high horsehide boots. It was gear for the wild country that lay between the Ranch of the Two Brothers and Blue Beach. He carried his best musket, his tinderbox, and his powder horn. I dressed accordingly, but carried no weapon except a knife.

There were four horses saddled and waiting for us. I rode my stallion, Tiburón, and I rode astride.

The river would still be running a torrent. It was much easier to cross close to the ranch and go down the south bank, but we had no desire to get soaked so early on the journey.

Accordingly, we chose the north bank and followed it through heavy chaparral and patches of cactus until we had ridden for two hours.

Where the river widened and ran knee-deep, we crossed to the south bank. It was still a good hour's ride from the Blue Beach. But it was here that we took the first precaution.

My father and I had been coming to Blue Beach for two years. On the three journeys we had made, we had always been followed. Sometimes by one or two Indians, sometimes by more. But to this day, no one had followed us farther than this west crossing. Here we had managed to elude them.

One thing that helped was that we never told anyone our secret — the story of the Blue Beach.

We told none of the vaqueros or the *mayordomo*. Nor Rosario, though Rosario could be trusted. Nor my sister, who could not be. Nor even Doña Dolores, whom we could trust most of all. Dolores you could hang by her thumbs and still not hear one word that she did not wish to speak.

There was no way to find the Blue Beach except by following the river, either down from the mountains or up from the sea. From the sea no one would ever find it because of a series of lagoons. From the direction of the mountains you would need to be very lucky, as lucky as we had been in the beginning.

The river at this point, where it fanned out into the deep lagoons, ran narrow, between two sheer walls of granite, where even a mountain goat would be lost. At the bottom of these cliffs were two beaches, one facing the other across a distance of a hundred steps.

The beaches were strips of fine sand, finer than

the sand you find on the sea beach itself. Both had a bluish cast, like pebbles you see through clear-running water. But they also had another color, a lighter blue that had a look of metal, as if there were copper deposits in the cliffs that had been washed down by the river and the rain and had mixed with the lighter color.

Someone might call the beaches green or the color of turquoise, but to us they were blue and this is what we called them — the Blue Beaches, more often, the Blue Beach.

On this day, as on the three other journeys we had made to the Blue Beach, we tied our horses and climbed up from the stream to a towering rock. This was where we took our second precaution, for from this high place we could survey the trails, one coming along the river, and one from the sea.

"What do you see?" my father said. He liked to test my eyesight. "Are we followed?"

"I see nothing on the trail," I said, "either from the river or from the sea."

"What is the brown spot among the oaks?"

"Where?"

"Up the river about a hundred *varas*."

"I see nothing."

"Look once more."

"Does it move?"

"Judge for yourself. But first you need to find it."

I looked hard and at last made out the brown spot among the oaks. "It is a cow grazing," I said.

"There are two, and one is not a cow but a yearling fawn. What do you hear?"

"The stream."

"What else?"

"A crow somewhere."

"Is that all?"

"Yes."

"Listen."

"A woodpecker behind us."

"Yes. And what else do you hear?"

"Nothing."

"Besides the stream and the surf at the mouth of the river and gulls fishing?"

"You have good ears."

"And you will have them someday."

"Never so good as yours."

"Better. *Mucho más.*"

Don Saturnino was silent for a while. Then he said, "Tomorrow is Carlos's birthday. He would have been eighteen had he lived."

"He would have liked these journeys," I answered.

"Perhaps. Perhaps not. Who knows? It is

sufficient that you like them. You do like them, Carlota?"

"Everything, Father," I said. "Everything."

Here we sat for an hour, to make sure that we had not been followed.

When the sun was overhead, we crawled down from the pinnacle. We reached the Blue Beach and took off our boots and stepped out into the middle of the stream. We made our way for a distance of some fifty paces, leaving no tracks behind us. A clump of willows grew amidst a pile of driftwood and boulders at this place. Here the river divided and ran in two smaller streams on both sides of the willows.

The boulders could not be seen at high tide. But the tide was low now and they stuck up in two crescents, facing each other and leaving a clear space between them. The water was cold, both the sea water that met the river at this point and likewise the river water itself.

Stripped to my singlet, I splashed water on my legs, on my arms and chest. I had found that the best way to approach cold water was by small shivers, suffered one at a time.

Throwing out my arms, I took in a great gulp of air, held it for a minute, counting each second. Then I let out all the air in a quick whoosh. Then I raised my arms again and took in a greater gulp.

27

This air I held for two minutes, still counting the seconds in my mind — one second, two seconds, and so forth. I repeated this three times. The third time I counted up to four minutes.

It had taken me two years to build up to where I could hold my breath for this length of time. My father had heard of pearl divers in La Paz who could hold their breath for five minutes and even longer. I had tried this but had fainted.

Carefully we stepped into the wide pool between the two crescents of stone, beneath the canopy of willows. We inched our way to the center of the pool, cautious not to rile the sand.

As my foot touched a smooth slab of stone, I stooped down, lifted it with much care, and set it to one side. Beneath it was a rock-lined hole filled with water, the size of my body and twice its height.

At the bottom of this hole was something that, when we first saw it, seemed to be the trunk of a tree — a tree washed down from the mountains. Undoubtedly, it once had risen above the water, but over the years floods had worn it away to a worm-eaten stump.

It had been the mainmast of a ship, which my father said was some seventy feet in length. It had the wide beam, the high stern, of the galleons that two centuries before had sailed the seas between

China and the coast of California and Mexico.

These ships, my father said, came on favorable winds and currents to northern California, then along the coast south to the ports of San Blas and Acapulco. They carried great treasures from the Indies, these galleons, so great that they became the prey of American and English pirates.

Some of these treasure ships had been captured. On some, their crews had died of scurvy. Others had run aground through careless navigation. Others were driven ashore by storms. Still others had sought refuge from their pursuers by hiding in lagoons such as the one at Blue Beach.

"This must have been a large lagoon at one time," my father said when we first discovered the galleon. "A good place to hide a ship. But when it was once inside, something happened to the ship and it never returned to the sea."

Hidden in the galleon's hold, near the stump of the mainmast, were two chests filled with coins. The coins were of pure gold. They showed three castles and the two flying doves that meant they had been struck in the mint at Lima, Peru. The date marked upon each coin that we carried away on the trips we had made was the year of Our Lord 1612.

The two chests — each made of hard wood banded with iron straps and sealed with a hasp that had rusted and fallen off — were well beneath the surface of the water, whether at low tide or in the summer, when the stream ran low. This was fortunate, for had the chests been exposed, some passing Indian or vaquero would have discovered them.

◄ · 5 · ►

There were many things to do before the chests could be reached. Usually it took me half a day to bring up a pouch of coins from the sunken ship.

The place where I dove, which was surrounded by jagged rocks and driftwood, was too narrow for my father. He had tried to squeeze through when we first discovered the galleon, but partway down he got stuck and I had to pull him back. It was my task, therefore, to go into the cavelike hole. My father stood beside it and helped me to go down and to come up.

I buckled a strong belt around my waist and to it tied a riata that was ten *varas* long and stout enough to hold a stallion. I fastened my knife to my wrist — a two-edged blade made especially for me by our blacksmith — to protect myself against spiny rays and the big eels that could sting you to death. In the many dives I had made, I never had seen a shark.

Taking three deep breaths, I prepared to let myself down into the hole. In one hand I held a sink-stone, heavy enough to weigh me down. I let out all the air in my chest, took a deep breath, and held it. Then I began the descent.

The sink-stone would have taken me down fast, but the edges of the rocky hole were sharp. I let myself down carefully, one handhold at a time. It took me about a minute to reach the rotted deck where the chests lay. I now had two minutes to pry the coins loose and carry them to the surface. We had tried putting the coins in a leather sack and hoisting them to the surface. But we had trouble with this because of the currents that swept around the wreck.

The coins lay in a mass, stuck together, lapping over each other and solid as rock. They looked, when I first saw them, like something left on the stove too long. I always expected to find them gone, but now as I walked toward the chests, with the stone holding me down, I saw that they were still there. No one had come upon them during the seven months since our last visit.

The first time I had dived and brought up a handful of coins, I said to my father that we should empty both the chests and take the coins home.

"Then everyone would talk," Don Saturnino said. "As soon as they saw the gold coins the news would spread the length of California."

"We don't need to tell anyone. I can hide them in my chest at home."

"The news would fly out before the sun set. At the ranch there are many eyes."

I still thought it was a better idea to empty the chests before someone else did, but I could see that my father enjoyed these days, when the two of us went to the Blue Beach, so I said no more.

The sun was overhead and its rays slanted down through the narrow crevice. There were many pieces of debris on the deck and I had to step carefully. With my knife I pried loose a handful of coins. They were of a dark green color and speckled here and there with small barnacles. I set the coins aside.

My lungs were beginning to hurt, but I had not felt the tug of the riata yet, the signal from my father that I had been down three minutes. I pried loose a second handful and put my knife away. Before the tug came I dropped my sink-stone and took up the coins. Gold is very heavy, much heavier than stones of the same size.

Fish were swimming around me as I went up through the hole of rocks and tree trunks, but I saw no sting rays or eels. I did see a shark lying back on a ledge, but he was small and gray, a sandshark, which is not dangerous.

On my third trip down, I hauled up about the same number of coins as the other times. The pouch we had brought was now full. I asked my father if we had enough.

"Are you tired?" he said.

"Yes, a little."

"Can you go down again?"

"Yes."

"Then go."

I dived twice more. It was on the last dive that I had the trouble. The tug on the riata had not come, but I was tired, so I started away from the chest with one handful of coins. Close to the chests, between them and the hole, I had noticed what seemed to be two pieces of timber covered with barnacles. They looked as if they might be part of a third and larger chest.

I still held my knife and I thrust it at a place where the two gray timbers seemed to join. It was possible that I had found another chest filled with coins.

As the knife touched them, the two timbers moved a little. Instantly, I felt pressure upon my wrist. I drew back the hand that held the knife. Rather, I tried to draw it back, but it would not move. The tide had shifted the timbers somehow and I was caught. So I thought.

I felt a tug upon the riata fastened to my waist.

34

It was the signal from my father to come to the surface. I answered him with two quick tugs of the leather rope.

Now I felt a hot pain run up my arm. I tried to open my fingers, to drop the knife, but my hand was numb. Then as I stared down into the murky water I saw a slight movement where my hand was caught. At the same moment I saw a flash of pink, a long fleshy tongue sliding along my wrist.

I had never seen a burro clam, but I had heard the tales about them, for there were many on our coast. Attached to rocks or timbers, they grew to half the height of a man, these gray, silent monsters. Many unwary fishermen had lost their lives in the burros' jaws.

The pain in my arm was not so great now as the hot pains in my chest. I gave a long, hard tug on the riata to let my father know that I was in trouble. Again I saw a flash of pink as the burro opened its lips a little, and the fat tongue slid back and forth.

I dropped the coins I held in my other hand. The burro had closed once more on my wrist. But shortly it began to open again, and I felt a sucking pressure, as if the jaws were trying to draw me inside the giant maw.

Putting my knees against the rough bulge of the shell, as the jaws opened and then began to close,

I jerked with all my strength. I fell slowly backward upon the ship's deck. My hand was free. With what breath I had I moved toward the hole. I saw the sun shining above and climbed toward it. The next thing I saw was my father's face and I was lying on the river's sandy bank. He took my knife in his hand.

After I told him what had happened, my father said, "The knife saved your life. The burro clamped down upon it. See the mark here. The steel blade kept its jaws open. Enough to let you wrench yourself free."

He pulled me to my feet and I put on my leather pants and coat.

"Here," he said, passing the reins of his bay gelding to me, "ride Santana. He goes gentler than Tiburón."

"I'll ride my own horse," I said.

"Good, if you wish it."

"I wish it," I said, knowing that he didn't want me to say that my hand was numb.

"Does the hand hurt?"

"No."

"Some?"

"No."

"You were very brave," he said.

My father wanted me to be braver than I was. I wanted to say I was scared, both when the burro had hold of me and now, at this moment, but I didn't because he expected me to be as brave as Carlos. It was at times like this that I was angry at my father and at my dead brother, too.

"It was good fortune," I said.

"Fortune and bravery often go together," Don Saturnino said. "If you do not hurt, let us go."

I got on the stallion and settled myself in the saddle. "Yes, let us go," I said, though I could not grip the reins well with but one hand.

On the way home we talked about the pouchful of coins and my father decided to sell them in San Diego. The first coins he had sold in Los Angeles to a gringo trader.

"The gringo was curious about where I got them," he said. "Too curious to suit my fancy."

"What did you say to him?" I asked.

"I said that the coins had been in the family for many years. He looked at them for a long time. He turned them over and over. He was curious about the green spots on the coins. He said the coins must have been in the sea at some time. I told him that it was likely, since my grandfather was a captain of the sea."

"I didn't know that my great-grandfather was a captain of the sea."

"He was not," Don Saturnino said, and laughed. "We will try San Diego this time. Doña Dolores

37

has invited the countryside, so we will need to make a good bargain. We will need to buy two barrels of *aguardiente* because all the Peraltas possess legs that are hollow. Some of the Bandinis and one or two of the Borregos, especially Don Alfonso Borrego, are hollow likewise."

My father also liked to drink the fiery *aguardiente*.

"And we'll have music?" I said.

"Much music. And not from Dos Hermanos. We will search and find the best from everywhere. We will make the Peraltas envious. And all the rest. We will dance for two days and not pause except to fortify ourselves."

We came to the brow of the hill that lies between Dos Hermanos and the sea. Below us, in front of the big gate of our half-house, half-fort, fires were burning in pits the Indians had dug. The fires would burn for three days, until the night before the wedding. Then a thick layer of ashes would be sprinkled over the coals, and slabs of beef, half a cow, each wrapped in heavy wet cloth would be laid on the beds and covered with earth. The slabs would cook and steam all night and most of the next day. Already I was hungry, thinking about the tender meat.

My father said, "Are you pleased that it is Yris who marries the Peralta?"

"Yes, very pleased," I said.

"You have no regrets?"

"None."

"Someday I will hunt and find you a suitable young man. He will likely come from the North, where the young men, I hear, are more handsome than here in the South. And we will have a wedding such as no one has seen before. Would that please you?"

"When do you hunt for the young man?" I asked.

"Soon. Very soon. Not later than next spring. It may take some time before I find him, of course. Perhaps a year or so."

"Of course," I said, having a deep misgiving about my father and this search.

"Handsome young men of good character do not grow upon trees. Yet I will look throughout California, from one end to the other. If I do not find him here I will look elsewhere, even in far-away Spain."

My hand hurt and that made things worse. But I was fortunate. I could have been back there on the rotting deck of the galleon, in the grip of the giant burro clam. I could be lying drowned beneath the waves. Or I could be at home, like Yris, getting ready to marry Don Roberto.

·6·

The weather was fine and the wedding guests came from all directions. They came in *carretas* drawn by oxen, on horseback with dogs at their heels, young and old, dressed in silver and brocades. The women smelled of perfume and the men's hair shone with bear grease.

By noon the hitching rack outside the big gate was full and we built another. Carts fanned out across the mesa. We had room in the house for thirty-two, about a fourth of the guests. The others raised colored tents around the house. In all, Doña Dolores had invited one hundred and twenty. All came, and many besides who were not invited.

Yris wore a dress of fine white muslin with knots of pink flowers around the hem. Her skin was pale because she never went out without a parasol when the sun was shining. She also wore a lot of white powder, which she had bought from a gringo trading ship. In her pale skin and white powder and pink and white dress, she looked like a delicious dessert, like one of the sugary *buñelos* that Anita, the cook, made.

Yris said to me, "I hope you aren't put out because I am marrying first. He is a fine and wonderful man."

"He is, and he is also the best horseman in the countryside," I said, thinking about a white gelding he owned, which I would like to trade a brood mare for when the wedding was over and he was my brother-in-law. Thinking, too, how fortunate it was that I would not need to wait on him as his obedient wife. "No, Yris, I am only envious of you."

"I am glad you do not mind," said Yris, looking at her hands. "It will be good to be mistress in my own household." She raised her eyes to the spot where Doña Dolores sat welcoming the guests, and it struck me stronger than ever how difficult it must have been for her, being, as she was, the daughter of my father's unlucky second wife.

Don Roberto wore his hair in the *furioso* style, pushed up in front and long on the sides. His jacket was made of black velvet tricked out with silver braid and large silver buttons. His trousers were split up the sides, and when he walked you could see flashes of red. I crossed myself. I thanked the Virgin Mary that it was Yris, and not I, Don Roberto was marrying.

41

Our chapel would hold only half of those who wanted to see the wedding, so it was held outside, by the corral. Father Barones came from Santa Ysabel to read the service. He was an old man and spoke in a quavering voice that no one could hear.

"Just as well," my grandmother hissed in my ear. "It is likely the wrong passage that he is reading from the Bible. When you are married, I will send to San Gabriel for Father Justo."

The musicians played many tunes during the wedding. There were five men and they played three guitars and two violas. When the wedding was over and one of the barrels of *aguardiente* was empty, everyone hurried down to the pits, where the cooks had uncovered the slabs of meat and placed them upon trestles.

My grandmother poured herself a handful of salt and dipped her meat into it. She always seemed to like the salt better than the beef. I think she ate the meat to enjoy the salt. Father Barones took some of the beans, some tortillas, and a scoop of chile and a slice of the beef. Then with his knife he stirred all the food together, round and round, before he spooned it up.

"He is very religious," my grandmother said. "He thinks it is a sin to eat good food, so he makes it look like something else."

I heaped my platter and ate where I couldn't

watch Father Barones. The beef was tender and sweet on the tongue.

In the afternoon, after a long siesta, everyone gathered on the mesa for horse racing and sports. I rode to the mesa on my gelding, Sixto, following my grandmother in her silk-lined *carreta*. Tiburón was too much for me to manage. My swollen hand still would not grip the reins. I could manage the gelding with spurs alone, but not the stallion, who required a heavy Spanish bit as well.

My grandmother said, "The way you are dressed you must plan to ride in the races."

I had on a deerskin shirt dyed blue and deerskin trousers and blue-stitched boots. I wanted to wear a pretty dress with ruffles, which Doña Dolores had bought for me from a Yankee trading ship, but my father said I looked better in trousers than I did in a dress. I didn't like this remark very much.

Doña Dolores gave up, saying, "The harm is already done. By now everyone knows Carlota de Zubarán. A little more cannot hurt." She dabbed at her eyes and gave a little sniff.

I did promise her that I would not go in the rooster race, which made her feel better, but not much. I failed to tell her that I didn't like the race, anyway.

This was a race between four men. Six roosters

were buried in the ground up to their necks, just their heads showing. Then the men set off at a gallop. The winner was the one who could reach the finish line first, with the most chicken heads in his hand. Sometimes there was a second race if it was a tie; even a third. It took a great deal of skill to reach down when the horse was at a gallop and at the right instant snatch off the rooster's head. My father was famous, I had heard, as a rooster racer when he was in his youth. I didn't like the race and never tried it. But it was very popular.

I took part in only one of the events. This one was for speed and endurance. The course started from the hitching rack. It ran for a league across the mesa and through a grassy marsh and up a rise and across a deep ditch and through some heavy chaparral and then back in a last straight run for the hitching rack.

I had an advantage because I knew the country, having traveled it many times. I was willing to give the rest of the riders a head start, but all of them, including the bridegroom, scoffed at the idea.

"I should give *you* a head start," Don Roberto said, casting a look at me, I am sure comparing me in my leather clothes with his beautiful white and pink bride. And I could hear him congratulating himself that it was a piece of good fortune that he had not married me. "Perhaps a hundred *varas*, halfway across the mesa," he went on. "I will advise the others."

"Don't bother, Brother-in-law," I said. "I'll race you even or not at all."

This did not please Don Roberto. Nor my father, who had bet heavily on the race and wanted any advantage for me that he could get. He said nothing, however, because he didn't want the men to feel that they were racing someone who needed a head start.

⊷ 7 ⊶

There were eleven riders in the race. The men were all young. I knew some of them by their first names. I was familiar with what their horses could do. If I had been able to ride the stallion I would have won easily. About the gelding, Sixto, I knew little, other than that he was easy to ride as long as he wasn't trailing the other horses.

My father bet all the coins he hadn't spent on the wedding, which were equal in value to three hundred cows and twelve riding horses.

"No mustangs," my father said to Don César, his dear friend with whom he was betting. "Horses of good breeding, not decrepit with old age. And the cows the same; no crow bait."

"But these coins," said Don César. "What are they?"

"Gold," Don Saturnino said.

"I know, but whence do they come?"

"From Spain," my father said, telling a lie. "*Verdad?*"

"*Es verdad.* Grandfather Don Sebastián was a minister of the King's treasury."

"Your grandfather stole them from the treasury?"

"Undoubtedly, my friend. As you would do had you but the opportunity."

As they shook hands on the bet, my father gave me a wink and so did Don César. They were good friends, but both of them liked to win. My father had advice for me as I drew up to the hitching rack and waited for the *alcalde* to drop his handkerchief for the start of the race.

"Hold back and let them all lead across the mesa. I will approach Don César again while you are riding last, and increase the bet. That way we may double our winnings."

"The gelding doesn't like to run last," I said. "He'll sulk and I won't able to handle him."

"Run in the pack, then," my father said, "but do not run first or second or even third."

"In the middle," I said.

The *alcalde's* red handkerchief fell to the ground. I spurred the gelding into a gallop, but as soon as he was underway I pulled in on the reins and fell back. Don Roberto passed me and said something that I didn't catch. He rode the fastest horse in the race, a black gelding his father had bought him as a wedding present. It was a five-year-old that had won many races around the pueblo of Los Angeles. Don Roberto was a good

47

rider, but it was the horse I had to beat.

The mesa was flat, with short-cropped grass, and sloped a little to the south. I was toward the last when we reached the trail that led steeply down into the river marsh.

I had been through the marsh when I had gone to the Blue Beach with my father. The shortest way across it was not through the center of the marsh, which was deep, but along the north edge, where the water was shallow. None of the riders knew this but me.

As we came to the marsh we were now out of sight of Don César and my father and everyone else. I touched the gelding with a spur, left the pack that was wading through the tules into deep water, and followed the north edge of the marsh.

Don Roberto perhaps thought that I was having trouble and was about to abandon the race. He raised a gloved hand toward me and shouted, "*Hola,* this way."

"*Hola,*" I shouted back, thinking that it was nice of him to be so considerate of me.

I reached the far side of the marsh before he did, before any of the other riders, including Don Palomares, who had been the King's soldier and was accustomed to marshes.

Don Roberto and the rest were now a hundred *varas* behind, too far away for me to shout "*Hola.*"

Halfway up the rise was a *zanja*, a ditch filled with water that came from the river and that we used to irrigate our garden of corn, frijoles, and chili. I could have jumped it with ease on Tiburón, but the gelding I was not sure of, so I waded through the ditch. This cost me time, for all the other riders jumped it except a boy I had never seen before, who landed on his back in the middle of the ditch.

At the top of the rise I was in the lead by more than a hundred *varas*. The gelding was running well and I was sure he had strength for the race across the mesa. He would not be so fast as Don Roberto's horse — no other horse in California del Sur was — so I needed a good lead to win.

◄ · 8 · ►

When we entered the chaparral I slowed Sixto to a *pasotrote,* the best gait for threading your way through the dense thicket of manzanita, ribbon-wood, and mountain mahogany. When I came near to the last of the chaparral, I used spurs on the gelding and he responded, raising his head and snorting.

Tiburón would have spied the coyote hole. He would have shied away from it and reared on his hind legs, as he sometimes did when he saw a tumbleweed coming toward him. Or when he came suddenly upon a coiled rattlesnake.

Sixto did not see the hole. Nor did I. I was glancing back at that instant to see where the other riders were. Sixto went into the hole with his left forefoot and lurched sidewise and came to a halt. I went over his head, and the next thing I knew I was lying in a thorny tangle.

Much of my breath had been knocked out of me, but somehow I managed to get on my feet. The gelding stared around, wild-eyed. He had a notion to bolt, leaving me there, shoulder-deep in

50

chaparral, but I went toward him slowly, and called his name softly. Fortunately, he was not hurt.

At the last moment, as the gelding was about to change his mind and bolt, I grabbed for the reins and caught them. I sidled over to a mesquite bush, got one foot in a stirrup, and swung up.

I flicked Sixto with the Spanish spurs, which had wheels bigger than my hand, and we went out, crashing through the last of the chaparral and onto the open mesa. I glanced back at the other riders, hoping that none of them had seen me fall. They were just coming into view.

I flicked Sixto again, this time with both spurs, and gave him all his head. I raised myself a little in the saddle and leaned low and far out over the gelding's neck. I could hear hoofs behind me now. I held my breath.

We were better than halfway across the mesa when I glanced over my shoulder and caught a glimpse of a silver-studded jacket and a flash of red pantaloons. Far off in front of me I saw a crowd in front of the big gate. Then I heard the sound of cheering.

The thud of hoofs was now close upon me. It could be no one except Don Roberto. In spite of his fat little hands he was a fine rider. How he would love to beat me! I still wondered if he had seen me tossed into the chaparral. It would be a shame to lose the race because of this mischance. A good horseman would never let his horse blunder into a coyote's hole.

The cheering grew louder. I could see my father now; at least the broad sombrero with the silver spangles on it. I thought I felt the hot breath of Don Roberto's horse. This could not be. It must be my own breath that I felt. Then I no longer heard the thud of hoofs. I glanced back, but Don Roberto was still there, not gaining on me, not losing either.

His horse came on steadily, close, closer, then even with my gelding's flank. I could have reached back and touched its nose. I could have given his horse a backhanded slap with my braided quirt. But I held the quirt in the hand the burro clam had injured.

"*Hola!*" shouted Don Roberto.

The shout seemed to sound in my ear, but I still was in the lead by half a length. The hitching rack was near. It was hidden by the guests, who were waving their hats and handkerchiefs. The race would not be decided until the horses were tied to the hitching rack. This meant that I must ride as close as I could to the rack and lead the horse the rest of the way. If I were riding Tiburón, this part would be easy.

The crowd began to scatter, leaving the space in front of the rack empty. Don Roberto's horse came up even with me. Don Roberto shouted words that I couldn't catch, but it was a taunt of some kind.

I made a tight half-circle and pulled up when I was still a dozen paces from the hitching rack. My gelding's hoofs slid on the loose earth and a small cloud of dust flew up and blinded me for a moment. I held the reins in my good hand and turned the gelding toward the rack.

Don Roberto had ridden a few steps past me. He brought his horse up stiff-legged, and was on the ground at once. There was a din of voices, but I made out my father's voice shouting, *"Andale, andale!"* at me.

Don Roberto would have won the race if his gelding had not reared as he jumped to the ground. I reached the hitching rack and tied the reins in a hard knot before he could quiet his horse. He smiled and held out his hand. I was surprised at what a nice smile he had. I had not noticed it before.

My father rushed over to kiss me. He put an arm around my shoulder and led me to where his friend Don César stood.

"When do you deliver the cows and horses?" my father said.

"How many did we wager?" Don César asked, as if he didn't know and didn't care.

"Twelve good riding horses," Don Saturnino said. "Three hundred and fifty cattle."

"Three hundred," Don César corrected him.

"Three hundred, but no boneyards."

I wondered what use we would have for three hundred cattle. We already had more than seven thousand. And a cow was selling for only fifty centavos. But Don César owned a herd of fine brood mares, and somehow I would try to get one or two. Perhaps we could trade some of the cattle or all of them for one good mare.

◄· 9 ·►

After the race the *alcalde* cleared everyone from
the field in front of the gate and ten of the young
men jousted with lances.

I was good with the lance — I had three of
them, all made of black walnut wood and tipped
with Toledo steel. I wanted to joust but my hand
would not stand the hard thrusts that were required, so I had to sit by and watch.

The *baile* that night was very pretty, with colored lanterns, which had been strung across the
courtyard, giving off a golden light, and the musicians, from their platform of pine boughs, playing
many *jotas* and Aragonese waltzes and *bambas*.

To please my grandmother I wore the dress she
had bought for me the year before. It was of black
bombazine with ruffles at the hem and cuffs and
neckline. I felt uncomfortable in it, used as I was
to the feel of leather. Two of the Yorbas and Doña
María of the Palomareses said it was very becoming to me. But none of the men said anything. I
think, perhaps, it was because I had beaten Don

Roberto in the race. Or just that for some reason they were afraid of me.

Anyway, I didn't dance much, except once with my father and once with Don Manuel of El Nido and once with Don Roberto, who, like me, was a better horseman than a dancer.

"I would like to race you again," Don Roberto said.

"It will be a better race if I ride Tiburón," I said.

"I would have won," said my new brother-in-law, "had my horse not balked at the last minute, just as I was reaching out to tie him. I don't like the tying. It is not good for true racing."

"I agree."

"Then we will race again?" Don Roberto said.

"Soon," I said, "and you will give me a handicap."

I thought this would please him, and it did.

"Fifty *varas*," he said, puffing out his round cheeks. "Unless you desire more."

"No. Fifty *varas* is sufficient."

I would tell my father so that he could make another bet with his friend César Peralta. In the meantime, there was something else.

Don Manuel of El Nido I had not met before. He had come after the games were over. His long sideburns were gray and he was handsome and a very good dancer. Once he had been a soldier in Spain, before the King gave him a grant of nine thousand acres to the south of our ranch. His wife had died on their way here, to New Spain, and he had not married again.

"I am sorry that I did not see you in the race this afternoon," he said. "It pleases me that you beat the young caballeros. An arrogant group. You gave them a good lesson, which they need and deserve. It surprises me, since they carry themselves with such airs and arrogance, why they do not go north to fight the gringo."

"That trouble is mostly over," I said.

"It would not be if they and others of their kind would give up their easy ways and take to the saddles. They act like children whose mothers still need to change their pants."

I wondered, because Don Manuel was once a soldier, why he did not take to the saddle himself. Then I thought that he must be like my father, like all the rest of the Spanish landholders, who were certain that the gringo would win the last battle. Should they oppose the Americans, they would end by losing their lands and perhaps their lives.

When I was dancing with Don Manuel I saw my grandmother watching us. She nodded her head in approval, and when the dance was finished and I went to sit with her, she asked me if I liked Don Manuel.

"He is so handsome," she said. "And he has a ranch with many rich acres of bottom land."

"He is twice my age," I said bluntly.

"No difference, my child," she said. "All the ages have their advantages."

The musicians struck up a *bamba* and drowned out the list of advantages possessed by Don Manuel. She changed the subject by giving me a nudge.

"Dance," she said. "Show the Yorbas and the Bandinis that you can do something besides ride a horse. Also Don Manuel."

I got to my feet. Rosario brought me a glass of water. I set it carefully on top of my head and began the slow steps of the *bamba*. Then someone brought a handkerchief with two corners tied together and placed it on the ground. As I danced I picked it up with my feet. I did this dance only once because my bones hurt from the fall I had taken in the chaparral thicket.

All the boys began to throw *cascarones* at me and the other girls — duck eggs filled with perfumed water, some with confetti — while we shouted with delight. Even Don Saturnino's eagle, who had been sitting quietly on his perch, began to scream.

It was a fine wedding. My sister, Yris, looked beautiful. She was happier than I had ever seen her, laughing and kissing everyone. And Don Roberto I liked much more than I had.

◄ · 10 · ►

Late that night, when most of the guests were asleep, a vaquero rode up to the gate. The gate was closed and he beat upon it until my father roused himself. I had stopped on my way to bed for a drink of water from our springhouse. I followed Don Saturnino and watched while he opened the big gate and let the vaquero in.

The vaquero was out of breath. "I come from Rancho El Cajón at the foot of the pass. Do you know Don Francisco, the patron?"

"Certainly, I know him," my father said, with impatience at being disturbed in the middle of the night. "Continue. This is not a social hour."

"Two days ago, at dusk, as the sun set," the vaquero said, "a band of Indians, perhaps from the Mojave tribe, came through the pass."

"Why would the Mojaves use the pass?" my father inquired. "Mojaves always come from the desert, through San Gorgonio."

"They could be one or the other," the vaquero said. "Piutes or the Mojaves."

"But Indians," my father said. "You are sure of that?"

"Indians," said the vaquero. "They came without women."

"Definitely Indians?"

"Yes, *seguro que sí.*"

"Without their women?"

"Without."

"Riding?"

"Riding. Two of the horses carried your brand."

My father turned to me. "Bring the young man a bowl of chocolate and a *buñuelo.*"

"Two of the latter," said the vaquero.

But when I returned with the food and drink, he had gone. Thudding hoofs on the trail grew faint and disappeared.

"He has ridden away to spread the word," Don Saturnino said. "But I think he spreads a rumor. I think the Indians have come to trade."

"The last time the Piutes came, they came to steal. They stole twenty-one of our good horses, including my best gelding, Chubasco."

"That is why I think that now they come to trade. And that they are not Mojaves, as the excited young man suggests, but Piutes."

"Do they come to return Chubasco, my black gelding?" I asked.

Piutes or Mojaves, unlike our California Indians, were a serious problem, so in the morning the men got together in the big *sala*. When they came out it had been decided that we, the de Zubaráns, would gather the vaqueros and accompany our guests to the western boundaries of the ranch, to the King's Highway, where they would be safe.

We had only four good muskets at Dos Hermanos, but the vaqueros fastened their long lances to the saddles.

← ·11· →

We rode to the King's Highway early the next morning. The sky was cloudy, and patches of pearly fog hung above the meadows. Some of the vaqueros rode in front of our guests, a long procession of horsemen and carts, and other vaqueros rode to the rear. I was near the front, with my father.

Beside the trail where the Road of the Two Brothers met the King's Highway stood a statue of Christ. The statue was made of wood and over it was a roof of pine boughs to protect it from the rain. Someone had picked a small bouquet of wildflowers and placed it at Christ's feet.

The horsemen and carts came up and gathered around the roadside chapel. Letting down the skirts of his robe, which he had tucked up around his knees as he rode, Father Barones left his burro to graze. He had opened his breviary and was about to speak when it happened.

We heard the sound of hoofs before we saw the gray figures come slowly through the fog. There were six of them, six tall figures slouched low over their saddles, like Piutes. They were now at the bottom of a grassy swale, and I could see only their heads and shoulders. Father Barones closed his breviary.

"Indians on a raid would not ride in the open," my father said.

"They look like Piutes," a vaquero said.

"They wear no feathers," someone said.

"That you cannot tell from here," my father said. "Also, I have seen Piutes without the feathers."

"The last time they came," a vaquero said, "they wore no feathers. That was in the year of forty-four, when they set the roof afire with lighted arrows."

The vaqueros went to their horses and took the muskets from the sheaths and stood beside the chapel. Everyone was silent.

The gray figures came out of the fog, riding slowly, with a clatter of harness and gear. They were now less than a hundred *varas* away. They were not Indians, but six young gringos.

Our procession had taken up all of the ground where the two roads met. A heavy growth of chaparral on the far side of the road made it impossible for the gringos to ride around us. They came to a halt.

The young man in the lead had a bony face and

long blond hair whitened by the sun. He was riding a small speckled pony and leading a bay *mesteño*. Burned on the *mesteño's* flank was the slash mark with a circle around it, the brand of Don César Peralta.

Don César saw the brand at once. He walked over to where the gringo sat astride the speckled pony.

"There are six of you," Don César said, "and you have twelve horses. The one you ride and the one you lead carry my brand. How many of the others? How many horses have you stolen?"

The young man took his time answering. "None," he said. His lips were cracked by the sun and he seemed to have trouble speaking. "We bought 'em all. Every one."

"Where?" Don César said.

"Down the road." The gringo spoke good Spanish.

The other gringos had come up now and sat lounging in their saddles. They looked like the first one, the one who was speaking. At first glance they might have been brothers. They all had bony faces and streaked hair and blue eyes that were red-rimmed.

Don César said, "At Rancho El Nido?"

"Name don't sound familiar, señor. Down the road, it was. Paid a hundred pesos for the lot."

"The horses carry the Peralta brand," Don César said. "If you bought them, you bought stolen horses."

"Anyhow, señor, we bought them, stolen or not."

Don César didn't believe the gringo. Nor did any of us. It was the way the gringos acted that made me doubt what they were saying.

The young man took up his reins. "We'll be moving on," he said. "We got a long ways to go."

"You do not go anywhere," Don César said, "until you hand over the horses you lead. The ones you ride, you can keep."

Don César repeated his offer.

None of the horses was worth much. And we had hundreds of them, though many were wild. But what he said to the gringos seemed fair to me.

Juan Palomares said, "We wish to get on the trail. I have much to do when I reach home. Give him the horses."

Matías Yorba echoed his words. As he spoke, the gringo put a spur to his horse and the horse jumped. Sixto was circling around and I had trouble handling him. The big horse reared and I brought him down and made way for the gringo. As he passed by, the gringo reached out and slapped Sixto on the flank.

"Pardon," the gringo said to me. "Pardon, *muchacho*."

I don't know whether it was that he had given the gelding a slap that made me angry or that he took me for a boy. My grandmother said afterward, when we got back to the ranch, that she didn't blame him for calling me a boy since, with my hair braided up under my sombrero, I looked like one.

I glanced at my father. He looked as angry as I was. With a quick motion of his hand he gave me a signal. I grasped the riata coiled beneath my leg.

Sixto had backed off when the gringo slapped him, and when he came down I turned the gelding. At the same time I unloosed the coiled riata. It was a good one, fashioned of eight strands of leather, and it had taken Sanchez, the saddler, more than a month to make. It was of deerskin and every inch had been carefully chewed by his wife until it was soft. It would handle a bull. It would handle two bulls, one at each end.

When the gringo was beyond me at a dozen paces or so, I let the riata go. It went out slowly at first. The loop was perfect and long. It gained speed and rose in a curve and settled over the gringo's shoulders.

I pulled up on the rope and gave it a double

hitch around the saddle horn and turned the horse down the trail. The gringo fell from the saddle. He lay sprawled on the ground. The riata was still around his shoulders and his arms were pinned to his sides. Before I let up, I dragged him twice his length through the grass. He got to his feet and freed his arms from the noose and I coiled the riata and hung it on the horn.

The other gringos began to laugh. They laughed while he got back on his pony. He put his hand on the rifle he carried alongside the saddle. I think that for a moment he thought of using it on me. His eyes ran over the vaqueros who were sitting with muskets across their laps. Then he cursed under his breath and headed his pony down the trail and the others followed. They let loose the stolen horses they were leading.

They went to the brow of the hill. There the first gringo stopped while his friends went on. He lifted his rifle and fired toward us. He was firing at the statue of Christ, not at us. He hit the statue and it fell to the ground.

Everyone was silent. Our vaqueros took up their muskets and waited for my father to speak. He turned and gave me a prideful glance for what I had done. *"Vámanos!"* he said. "Now let us go and punish them."

Father Barones had picked up the statue. Its head had been splintered by the gringo's bullet. He stood in the way of the vaqueros, holding the broken statue in his arm.

"Let them go," he said.

12

The story about the Piutes had been true after all.
They attacked a ranch near the pueblo of Los
Angeles, burned a house, and rode off to the desert with a large herd of cattle and some good
horses.

That was the news until a short time after the
wedding, when Don Manuel Ybarra of El Nido
sent word that he wanted to call upon us to offer
his thanks for the charming hours he had spent at
the *baile*. But my grandmother looked upon this
as something else, something of far more importance than a polite visit.

We were sitting in the courtyard, drinking our
morning chocolate, when a vaquero from El Nido
rode in with Don Manuel's note. My grandmother
opened it with trembling fingers. She read the
note twice. Then she looked up and smiled. A
smile so early in the morning, or at any time for
that matter, was unusual for Doña Dolores.

My father and I looked at each other, and wondered. Doña Dolores then read the note to us and

put it away in the sleeve of her dress.

"I am pleased to know," she said, "that our Carlota made such a favorable impression upon Don Manuel."

"What makes you think that Don Manuel pays us a visit for that reason?" my father said. "It is the custom of Spain to make such a call. It is Spanish politeness that will bring him."

"Politeness, no doubt," Doña Dolores said, "for Don Manuel is a gentleman of breeding. But he is also a gentleman of the finest perceptions." She paused to glance at my dusty boots, at my hair pushed up under the sombrero. "He is also a gentleman of understanding."

"Don Manuel Ybarra of Rancho El Nido," my father said bluntly, as was his manner, "is old enough to be Carlota's father. Upon second thought, he is old enough to be her grandfather."

Doña Dolores snorted. Cigarillo smoke spurted from her nostrils.

"It will take a man of Don Manuel's years, of long experience, to manage your daughter," my grandmother said. "Furthermore, an officer in the King's army, who is accustomed to the deployment of troops in battle, of battles in all weather and in all circumstances."

"I will send Don Manuel a note in reply," my father said. "I will send it today, now. But as for encouraging him as a suitor for Carlota's hand, that I refuse."

Don Saturnino was faithful to his promise. Before noon he sent off a vaquero with a message to Rancho El Nido. He sent off two vaqueros, in fact. The other vaquero carried a note to Don César Peralta, requesting the cattle and horses he had lost on the race and agreed to deliver.

Don César answered the note. Toward the end of the week his vaqueros brought in three hundred cattle, part steers and part cows, and twelve horses. Of the horses, one was a fine breeding mare.

Don Saturnino decided to turn the cattle out to pasture without changing the brands. But the horses were more valuable, especially the mare.

"We'll make a brand that will fit Peralta's circle," my father said. "A small Z, smaller than the one we use."

Our blacksmith worked through the morning and made a brand that was half the size of my palm. We tried the iron cold and were satisfied that it would fit the Peralta circle nicely.

I never helped brand cattle, but I always helped with the horses, because we marked only those we valued. We did the branding in the small corral, which was near the hitching rack and the big gate.

It was late afternoon. There was a breeze from the sea but it was still hot on the mesa, and the dust the horses were kicking up stung my eyes. I pulled the bandana up over my nose and that helped me to breathe. I was sweating, and thinking how good it would be when we finished with the branding and I could ride down to the stream and bathe in the cool water.

I heard a voice behind me. My father had tied the breeding mare César Peralta had sent — I am sure he sent the mare because he knew that I would be pleased with her. And I had just lifted the hot branding iron from the fire and was taking the few short steps to where the mare lay when I heard the voice. I didn't know who it was, nor did I care, but when I heard the voice again I looked up.

It was Manuel Ybarra from El Nido and he was leaning on the top bar of the corral, watching me.

The iron was cherry red so I didn't stop to wave a greeting to him. I took a careful sight with the brand, aimed at the small Z at the center of the Peralta circle, over the slash mark, pressed it down firmly, and counted three seconds, as the hair sizzled and smelled strong.

The mare staggered when Don Saturnino released her and then began to gallop around the corral. Our brand looked handsome on her flank.

She would be the mother of many fine colts, I thought, and I gave her the name Gavilán Azul, Blue Hawk, because she had a bright hawklike look in her eyes and her coat was of bluish cast.

I waited for my father and we went over to speak to Don Manuel. He looked fresh and handsome, as if he hadn't ridden for two leagues over a dusty trail. He wore an officer's uniform, blue with scarlet edgings, and on his chest were five medals, each polished and bright. I hadn't noticed when we were dancing together at the *baile* that he had a deep scar on his cheek. It gave him the look of a warrior.

He glanced at me as if we had never met and then I was aware suddenly that he didn't recognize me in my working clothes. Not until I spoke did he take off his officer's cap and try to grin and make a bow while standing on the bottom pole of the branding corral, which is difficult.

We strolled into the courtyard, where my grandmother joined us and we all drank cool drinks made of cherimoya juice and honey. My grandmother kept telling Don Manuel nice things about me — how well I sewed — I had made the shirt I was wearing — and that I was a very good cook, that I was a thoughtful granddaughter.

While she was telling Don Manuel these nice things, he kept glancing at my boots and my grimy hands, and at the hair that was tucked up under my sombrero.

When the three of them forgot about me and were talking together, I slipped away and washed my hands and face and put on a pink dress and a pair of new pink shoes. But when I returned Don Manuel didn't notice me. He quietly drank his cherimoya juice, and when my grandmother asked him to stay to dinner — we were having quail and venison — he thanked her, but said that since he was still unfamiliar with the trail he must leave before dark.

No importa. It was of no importance that Don Manuel was going home before dinner. I had put on my pink dress and pink shoes mostly to please my grandmother. I wondered why a grown man like Don Manuel would go around showing off a chest covered with ribbons and medals.

He was no sooner on his horse and moving off across the mesa than Doña Dolores said to my father, "Why was it necessary to brand the horses on this day, on this day of all days?"

"Because the horses were in the corral and I wished to brand them before we put them out to pasture."

My grandmother thought for a while. "Why was it necessary for Peralta to send the horses today?" she said suspiciously.

75

Don Saturnino, who, as I have said, often spoke bluntly, said, "Don César Peralta sent the horses today because I asked him to send them today. Does that answer your question?"

Then my grandmother threw up her hands and asked God to be a witness to the dastardly act of an ungrateful son. She also asked Him to bear with me until I somehow learned to mend my errant ways.

◄ · 13 · ►

The gringos on the stolen horses we did not see again or hear of, but when summer ended and we were trying tallow at Dos Hermanos, two more came to the ranch. They were dressed in blue uniforms and one, who rode a spotted horse, called himself Lieutenant Carson. He came to buy jerky and yucca cakes for a long journey.

My father would not have let them through the gate if he had been home, but he was away in the pueblo. I told my grandmother what the men wanted.

"Give them all they ask for," she said, "but do not take money."

Doña Dolores didn't like the gringos any more than the rest of us did, but she thought it was a good idea to be on the safe side.

"The war is finished," she said, "and the gringos have won. California belongs to them now, but we still have our land. We will keep it if we keep our tempers and our manners."

"Have you forgotten the gringo who shot and broke the statue?" I said.

"I have not forgotten," my grandmother said.

The gringo who called himself Lieutenant Carson was very polite. He told me he was married to a Spanish girl who lived in Taos, a pueblo far away to the east of California.

"I haven't seen her for almost two years now," he said, "but I hope to see her soon. I am taking a message to President Polk that the fighting is over, and maybe I'll stop in Taos on the way and pay her a visit."

He used Spanish well for a gringo and he had a soft voice and a pleasant way of talking.

"Many people call me 'Kit.' Kit Carson. My friends call me 'Bub.'"

I gave him a double supply of jerky, a leather *bota* packed with strips of dried deer meat, since we had no yucca cakes, and when he wanted to pay me I refused the money, as Doña Dolores had instructed me to do. I thought soldiers always saluted, but when he rode away he tipped his hat and said politely, *"Vaya con Dios."*

I thought it was nice of him to hope that I would go with God. He was different from the man I had lassoed. This confused me, but not for long.

Lieutenant Carson was wrong about the war in California. And so was my grandmother. The most important battle of all the fighting in California was yet to take place. The battle came about in this way.

My father was gone from Dos Hermanos for almost a month. When he returned (we said nothing to him about the gringos who had come to the ranch) he brought with him the startling news that an army of American soldiers was on its way to California. Spanish travelers had passed the army camped west of Santa Fe and learned that it was headed toward San Diego and the pueblo of Los Angeles. As we learned later, the Americans thought that the war in California was still going on.

"The travelers arrived in Los Angeles with this word," Don Saturnino said. "They report that the army is small, not many more than a hundred gringos, but it is an army with rifles and cannon."

"More rumors," Doña Dolores said. "If it is true, which I doubt, what difference will an army make? We may never see it."

"An army devours all the countryside," Don Saturnino said. "It will ruin Dos Hermanos. Burn our buildings, kill our cattle, steal our horses."

"What do we do?" Doña Dolores was calm. "What?"

"We oppose the gringos."

"With what? Rusty muskets? A few lances? What miracle has taken place that permits us to fight an army when before we could not fight a few wandering bandits?"

Don Saturnino went to the window, where he stood with his hands clasped behind him. "We will oppose the gringos," he said, "so long as our weapons last."

"It is pride that speaks," my grandmother said. "It leads you down a dangerous path. It is best that you do not ride out to confront an army, even a small one. It is better that you remain here on our lands, attend to your own business, and pray for God's protection."

Don Saturnino made a loud sound in his throat.

"You will find that our neighbors agree that caution is wise."

"Caution!" my father shouted. "Cowardice!"

The words hung in the air. My father began to stride back and forth, his iron spurs clinking on the beaten floor. Suddenly he stopped and raised clenched hands.

"Beware!" he cried. "Beware!"

With this threat he left the room, slamming the heavy door behind him. He went at once to the armory, and there he remained for the rest of the day. I brought him dinner, which he did not eat. And supper, which he treated likewise. My heart went out to him. The gringos had come like summer locusts. Dos Hermanos would change. Our lives would change, whatever we did and however we felt. This was what most of our neighbors believed and I believed also. An army of gringos was a new danger, but my father, one Spaniard, a hundred Spaniards, could not stop them. It was only pride, as my grandmother had said, Spanish pride that blinded him.

She also said, while the two of us were sitting at the supper table, "If Don Saturnino persists in this folly, one day soon we shall be eating our soup with a fork."

The next morning my father gave orders to dig three pits. Into them the Indians threw collected refuse from the barnyard and the house.

"It will be a month until the pits yield saltpeter," he said. "We have ample supplies of charcoal and sulfur, but without saltpeter we cannot make good gunpowder. Therefore, we may need to rely upon the lance. First, however, we attend to the muskets. The gringo carries a rifle. It shoots straight and far. As you will remember from the morning on the trail. Thrice as far and many times as accurate as our musket."

We spent the next two days in the armory.

There were four muskets in the racks, but all of them were in poor condition. We cleaned the barrels with a wiping stick wrapped in a rag that had been soaked in deer fat. Then my father showed me how to adjust the triggers and set them to a feather touch.

In the side of each musket stock was a brass lid. Inside the lid was a patch box, which held twenty small pieces of linen. These we took out and carefully cleaned. Next we cleaned the powder flasks, which were made from black buffalo horn shaved thin as glass so you could see through them. Then we examined the flints and replaced several. The lances were oiled and the points sharpened with a stone.

While these preparations went on, and we waited for further news of the gringo army, many ranchers came to Dos Hermanos to talk to my father. Most of them thought that it was wise to remain quietly on our lands, to do nothing to goad the enemy. I hoped they would persuade my father against committing a rash act. But their advice he did not heed.

"We will give the gringos a lesson," he would say over and over.

I was greatly disturbed, for he wished me to feel as he did, as my brother Carlos would have felt, and I could not betray his trust.

⟵ · **14** · ⟶

Winter was early that year. The first cold came in November and killed our gardens. On the day of the cold, word came that the American Army was marching up from the desert and would soon be in the mountains.

The word was brought by one of the sheep-herders, who had been tending our sheep there in the Oriflames. We sent the flocks with him every year when the grass grew thin at Dos Hermanos. While he was cooking his breakfast, he looked down into the pass that snakes up from the desert and saw something move through the tall mesquite. He watched closely and made out that it was a company of horsemen carrying rifles across their saddle horns.

We were out at the pits early in the morning, my father and I, turning over the refuse to see if the crystals of saltpeter had begun to form, when the sheepherder rode up. He had left the sheep with his son in a meadow two hours' ride from Dos Hermanos, and hurried on to bring us the news.

"How many horsemen did you observe?" my father asked him.

The sheepherder could not count. Instead, he made a wide gesture meaning many. "They came in a long line, señor, one following the other. Many of them, on thin horses. They also carried a flag."

"Not Spanish."

"Of blue and white and red."

"On the trail that leads to the hot springs?"

"Yes, on that trail, señor."

"Where they will camp, no doubt."

"It seems possible, señor. At the springs."

"While you watched them climbing the trail that leads to the springs did they observe you?"

"No, señor. I lay on my stomach among the rocks and watched with great caution."

My father sent the sheepherder back for the flock and rounded up three of our vaqueros. He gave one of them a message in writing to take to Don César Peralta.

"Go with a fresh horse for your return," he said to the vaquero. "And return without fail before night."

The other two vaqueros he also sent off with messages and fresh horses to the ranches of Don Baltasar Roa and Don Pedro Sanchez.

"Bring me their answers by tomorrow's dawn,"

he said. "Also without fail. We prepare a surprise for the gringo."

We went to the armory and again saw that things were in order. We had found little saltpeter in the pits, so there was no chance now to make powder for the muskets. Nor could we borrow any in the countryside, for none existed.

"It is no disaster that we cannot use the muskets," my father said. "The lance will not fail us. You and I are acquainted with the lance, are we not?"

"We are," I said.

"It is especially you who are familiar with the lance. I started you young with the lance; indeed, as soon as you could ride without holding to leather. At six, as I remember. You could have won at the wedding had you wished."

I stood holding tight to my favorite willow lance tipped with Toledo steel. I put it away in the rack and turned around to face my father.

"You intend for me to be with you against the gringo?"

He seemed surprised that I could ask the question. "Where else would you be at a time such as this?"

"What will the men say? Don César and Don Baltasar and the rest?"

"It does not matter what they say. We fight for

honor and our lives, not for their plaudits. We will need every lance we can muster."

The lance to me had been something for use in games, in mock battles on horseback against friends, not for use against an enemy, even a gringo enemy. Besides, it angered me that my father thought that my life was his to direct. But I held back my feelings.

"What was the message you sent?" I said.

"The message was brief. I told them what the sheepherder reported. To meet here tomorrow night. To bring their weapons."

"What if they do not come?"

"There is not one who will not come."

"We do not know for certain whether there is an army at the gate," I said. "The sheepherder could be wrong. Or the horsemen he saw could be a company of fur traders."

"Fur traders do not come in great numbers with rifles across their laps and a flag flying. And that many Spaniards are not on a journey."

Then we went to breakfast, but I wasn't hungry. "My *cuera*, my coat of bullhide, is not in good shape," I said. "It needs stitching."

"Then I will have it stitched and an extra layer of hide will be added. I notice that you do not eat."

"I have no hunger."

"Many times I feel that way myself," my father said. "Without hunger. The last time was when I went in pursuit of the Piutes. We rode to the big river and hid our horses in a cottonwood thicket and poled out to an island in our bull boat. We made a fine fire of driftwood. We had roasted venison over the coals on willow sticks we had peeled, when Don César said, 'Indians.' Just that: 'Indians.' I looked up and there they were, in war feathers, on the riverbank. They had come from somewhere and found our horses in the thicket. They were sitting on the horses now, watching us. I had a piece of venison to my mouth, ready to bite, and I dropped it in the sand. Suddenly, I had no hunger."

My father helped himself to a dipper of frijoles and peppers. "But fear, if you live, you get over. If you do not live, it does not matter." He looked up and smiled. "Now eat your frijoles, Carlota. They are tasty with the peppers."

I ate the frijoles but still I had no hunger.

← · **15** · →

The Peraltas, father and son, answered my father's message. They came that night and we talked until late. The next morning Fernando Soto came. Then that afternoon a vaquero rode in from the Sanchez ranch, which was near Los Angeles, with the news that Señorita Rosa María Sanchez planned to marry a young man named John Harper, a gringo. The vaquero brought the regrets and good wishes of her father, Simón Sanchez.

Don Saturnino groaned at this news and struck his forehead and walked around in a fury, but a little later that afternoon two young men came from the Montoya ranch, leading fresh horses and carrying lances. Though we had never seen them before, we had heard their names. They brought news that Americans were camped in the Oriflame Mountains. One of their vaqueros had made a count; there were one hundred and ten of the enemy. They were camped in a meadow beside a spring and were feasting on roasted sheep.

"We have nine lancers altogether," Don Roberto said. During our talk the night before,

Don César and Don Saturnino had placed him in command of our party.

"He is a fine horseman, though not so good in the saddle as you, Carlota," my father had said. "He is also brave. We will require both."

That afternoon another ranchero rode in from the coast, bringing with him two of his vaqueros. When we left the ranch at dusk there were twelve of us with lances.

My father said nothing to Doña Dolores about the gringos camped at the springs. Nor did I. She was in the *sala* and Rosario was kneeling in front of her when we went to say farewell. She did not look up. She was making one of her cigarillos. She took her time and folded the husk lengthwise and filled the crevice with tobacco. Then she spread the tobacco evenly and made a dimple in the center and used both her thumbs to tuck in the edge of the husk.

Only then did she glance up at my father, holding the half-rolled cigarillo in her hands. She gave Rosario a nudge with her toe and he ran to fetch her a coal. Only when she had licked the edges of the cornhusk and lit the cigarillo did she speak.

"Go," she said, "and get yourselves killed, you and your iron-headed daughter. I would not prevent it if I could."

"Señora Doña Dolores," my father said, "we

accept your blessings with gratitude. In return we extend our blessings to you."

He started to back out of the room, but Rosario jumped up and shouted, "Take me with you. *Por favor*, I —"

"No," my grandmother cried. "Never! They go but you stay. I need you."

Don Saturnino said to Rosario, "It is your duty to take care of the eagle and Señora Doña, in that order."

He left the room quickly and I followed him. I don't think my grandmother was as angry as she appeared to be, for when we rode away she stood at her window and waved us goodbye. I think she was as confused as I was. It was my father who lit the flame and kept it burning, out of anger and Spanish pride.

The war was really over. And in California it had never been a real war. In other places, but not here among the Californians. We all hated the men who ruled us from Mexico City and we would have revolted against them if the gringos had just left us alone to go our way. But now, as we were to learn later, General Kearny and his soldiers did not know that the war in California was finished. It was a misfortune that they didn't know.

The twelve of us took to the trail at dusk. There

was an early moon and we rode by its light until we came to Aguanga, which is a small Indian village about five leagues from the springs where the gringos were camped.

Here we ate our supper of jerky and yucca cakes. The night before, the chief of the Indians told us, gringos had come looking for horses and had driven off a dozen of his *mesteños*.

"They are getting ready to go somewhere," he said. "They have been resting at the springs, eating much, gathering horses. We have watched them. They will go soon, perhaps tomorrow."

Late that night, while we were sitting by the fire and talking, a party of rancheros rode in. They had gathered at San Juan Capistrano two days before. They had heard that we were on the trail and had followed us. Their leader was a lithe young man named Andrés Pico, the son of the Mexican governor of California, Pío Pico. There were twenty-one in his party and each man carried a lance.

It was agreed between Don Roberto and him that we would remain two parties, but that Pico would be in command when we met the gringos.

While we were sitting by the fire, off to ourselves and talking, my father said, "All of the men in our party know you. And the new ones, those who have come now with Pico, have heard of you.

Do not worry, therefore, about this business, about anything."

I was wearing my deerskin trousers and jacket. My long hair, braided and held with iron pins, was bound in a black handkerchief and pushed up under my hat. I looked like a boy but I didn't feel like one.

"I do not worry," I said, to make him feel happy.

We had heavy ponchos and we slept with them over us, with our saddles for pillows. The earth was hard. Many times in the night I wished that I were in my bed at home.

Early in the morning Don Andrés Pico and Don Roberto sent three Indians on fast horses to Agua Caliente, where the gringos were camped. The Indians came back at noon and reported that the gringos were marching down the valley, westward toward the sea, with flags flying. Some of their horses were fresh but many were thin and stumbling. That all the soldiers carried long rifles and the officers carried pistols and swords. They were also dragging two small cannon.

"We could use a dozen rifles," Don Andrés, the captain, said.

"How about the swords?" someone asked.

"And the pistols?"

"How about a cannon?"

"Even so much as a flag?"

"You will catch flies in your big mouths," Don Andrés said, "as well as other things. We have no rifles or pistols or swords or cannon. We *can* have a flag. Make one, Señorita Carlota, out of this." He took off his green scarf and tossed it to me. "We will have a flag and for every man a lance and some to spare. Be content."

To the mutter of leather and the song of metal crickets many of the horses wore on their headstalls, carrying the green flag I had made, we rode down the valley in a direction close to the one the gringos had taken. Most of the rancheros had silver on their bridles and pommels and their hooded stirrups. Andrés Pico had silver everywhere, even on the broad band of his sombrero.

We rode at a quick trot through the mist, down the valley between the dripping trees, on our way to intercept — that was the word my father used — to cut off the gringo soldiers at San Pasqual. It was the first time since the day word had come about the gringos, since the hour that we had left Dos Hermanos, that I felt good. It was exciting to ride through the mist, with the sound of hoofs and the jingle of harness. Though no one was watching, it was like riding in a parade.

◆· 16 ·◆

Late in the afternoon it began to rain, a soft rain
from the sea. We pulled our sombreros down over
our eyes and huddled deep in our ponchos. The
green flag got wet, and hung down from its staff
like a string.

The canyon that ran westward out of the
meadow was heavily wooded and narrow. A
stream ran through it and this we followed. Where
the canyon suddenly widened we found two old
shacks connected by a *portale* that the Indians
had abandoned. Here we tethered our horses and
made ready for the night.

One of the men had lassoed a wild goat on our
way down the canyon, so we all looked forward to
something besides the jerky we had been eating.
Vaqueros brought in armloads of dead manzanita
roots and made a fire out of the rain under the
portale.

My father skinned the goat and twisted the hind
legs, folding them over the back, the front legs
over the head. The whole thing he firmly worked

down on a skewer, solid and flat. Then two vaque-ros squatted opposite each other and turned the goat slowly over the fire.

The Indians came riding into our camp while the goat was roasting. They brought word that the gringo soldiers were camped nearby, some in small tents and others without tents.

"How far?" Don Andrés Pico said.

"Close," both of the Indians answered.

"How long on a horse?"

"Part of a morning," one of the Indians said.

"What part? Large or small?"

"Small," both of the Indians said.

We were all sitting around the fire, trying to dry out.

Don Roberto said, "The two trails, the one we traveled and the one the gringos travel, join here at the head of the meadow. The gringos are on their way to San Diego. They will need to pass this place to get there."

"Yes, there is no other trail," my father said. "They must pass here. They have no choice."

"But what if the gringos are not going to San Diego?" Don Andrés Pico said.

"Where else?" my father said. "They do not travel just to travel. They are on their way some-where. That place must be San Diego."

95

"There are American warships in the harbor at San Diego," one of the rancheros said. "They are going there to meet the ships."

"They could be going to pueblo Los Angeles," Don Andrés said.

"Not on this trail," my father answered. "From the springs they would have gone northward if they were going to the pueblo."

"What happens if they want us to think that they are going to San Diego when they are not? When they are really going to Los Angeles or somewhere else? To Santa Barbara, perhaps."

It was not settled where the gringos meant to go, but it *was* settled that they would need to pass the place where we were now camped. There was no other way out of the mountains.

My father scraped some fat from the goathide and fastened it on a stick and held it in the fire until it blazed. He then put the fat over the turning goat and let it dribble and spread. The meat grew brown and crackled and gave off little spurts of fire.

The rain had ceased but wet fog had come. We could not see much beyond the ring of the fire. When the goat was done, each of us took our knife and cut off a slice of meat. None of the men stood aside for me. I took my place with the others at the feast, which made me feel better. But no one had remembered to bring salt, so the meat tasted flat. It was good that my grandmother was not there.

One of the vaqueros thought he heard something and got up and left the fire. He was gone for a while and came back and said, *"Nada,"* and sat down.

"I would like to send someone up the trail to see what goes on with our gringo friends," Don Andrés said. "But he could lose himself in the fog and fall into trouble."

"They are where the Indians said they were," Don Roberto said. "They do not like the fog much either."

"They see no better in the fog than we," my father said.

"It would be good, however, to know," said Don Andrés. "And perhaps from that what they intend."

That night we kept the fire burning because it was cold. About midnight we all heard sounds in the brush. Two of the vaqueros and an Indian went out to look around. They were gone a long time, but when they came back they said they had found no signs of the enemy. We later learned that General Kearny had sent out a party to scout our camp. The sounds we heard in the brush were made by gringo scouts.

When the vaqueros who went to see about the sounds came back, Don Andrés got to his feet. He was tall and thin and had a pigtail, which he bound in a handkerchief. He looked serious in the firelight. He waited until everyone had quit talking.

He said, "We have been two parties. Now we are one and I am the leader of the one. My commands are to be obeyed promptly, without fail. Our lives and our fortunes depend upon it. The gringos will march in the morning, whether at sunup or afterward there is no telling. We are to be prepared for both, all gear in readiness, the horses fed and saddled. Juan Aguilar carries a musket, which he can use if the opportunity arises. The rest of us will rely upon our lances."

He stopped to listen and we waited. One of our horses had gotten loose and was wandering around in the fog.

Don Andrés said, "We are outnumbered four to one. We must, therefore, strike fast and then retreat. Then turn at my signal and attack again, then again retreat. I have no need to tell you how to use the lance; being Spaniards, you know already. But it is well to remember that you ride low, in the fashion of the Indians, and strike for the body, for the body alone. Two quick thrusts, more if possible."

I was sitting across the fire from Don Andrés. Suddenly I felt cold though the logs were glowing hot.

"Señorita," he said, looking down at me, "there are seven horses to spare. These we will tie and put in your hands. You are to remain with them at a place I will show you in the morning."

My father sat next to me, muffled in his poncho. He groaned as Don Andrés spoke to me. He was thinking of Carlos. He was sad beyond the use of words that his son was not there beside him, waiting for the dawn and the battle.

Overhead the fog had lifted a little. I could see racing clouds and a few stars. I was scared. I wondered if everyone else was scared, too.

·◄ 17 ►·

Dawn broke slowly. A cold breeze moved through the brush, but the valley below us was shrouded in mist. We had kept logs burning through the night and, having saddled the horses and put everything in readiness, we waited around the fire.

Don Andrés said to me, pointing down the valley, "Over against the hill is a clump of oaks." He waited until I made them out through the mist. "Take seven horses and ride now and quickly. Tether the horses there, in the trees, as much as possible out of sight of the enemy."

He paused and glanced over at my stallion. "It might be better if you ride something easier to handle. One of the spare geldings, say."

"I can handle the stallion," I said.

"In battle?"

"Anywhere," I said, though I was not sure. "In battle or out of battle."

"Very well," Don Andrés said, giving me a curious look. *"Buena suerte."*

"Thank you, sir, for your wish of good luck," I said.

"*Por nada*," Don Andrés said.

The seven horses we tied one to the other. I said goodbye to my father and led the horses at a quick trot out of the camp to the clump of trees against the hill.

The sun shone somewhere beyond the mountain rim, but here below, the mist was cold and heavy. I sat on Tiburón and kept my eyes on the place, which was close by, where the trail led out of the canyon. Far off I could see the fire of our camp and the men standing around it.

I heard no sound, nothing, as the first gringo rode out of the brush. He was seated on a small gray horse and he had braid on his hat and on his shoulders. He held the reins in one hand. A scabbard and sword hung from his saddle horn. I had no idea then, as he rode slowly past me, that he was General Kearny of the American Army.

From where I stood under the oak trees on a little rise, the valley stretched before me. On my right hand was the narrow ravine down which General Kearny came and his officers and men would come. The ravine led into a valley, off to my left, that was about three leagues in length and about a league in width, shallow and rolling. A stream that wandered through it was marked by willows and sycamore trees.

Across the valley, where we had camped that

night, I saw our men run for their horses. Before the officer on the gray gelding had gone more than a dozen steps, they rode out of the camp and raced at a hard gallop away from him, down the valley.

More officers now came into view, riding in single file. Among them I recognized the man on the spotted horse who had stopped at Dos Hermanos, Lieutenant Carson.

With Don Andrés and Don Roberto in the lead, our men were fleeing. Or so I thought. I guess that the gringos thought so too, for at once they set off in pursuit.

By now the first of the soldiers had ridden out of the canyon. Their horses looked scrawny and tired. The soldiers stopped to gaze at the valley, then at their officers in pursuit of the fleeing Californians.

But as the soldiers stood there at the mouth of the ravine, the Californians suddenly turned and rode back, still at a gallop, in a wide sweep along the far side of the valley, near the hill that was covered with cactus. This proved to be a ruse. It was to make the gringos think that our band was in flight.

The gringo officers pulled up their horses, not knowing what to expect. They did not know whether to follow the Californians or to stand where they were.

Then the Californians wheeled and galloped down upon the standing officers. I heard the voice of Don Andrés Pico. "Santiago and at them!" he shouted. It was the battle cry of the Spaniards who drove the Moors from Spain.

A gringo captain yanked at his sword, but he found that the sword was rusted in its scabbard. He drew a pistol and shouted to the officers who stood facing the oncoming lancers. I heard the thud of a musket, the one that belonged to Martinez. The shot struck the captain and he fell from the saddle.

I saw Lieutenant Carson, the man who had come to the ranch asking for food. He raised his rifle to use as a club. General Kearny who stood near him was struck by a lance and dropped to the ground. Most of the gringo officers were now on the ground, pierced by the steel-tipped lances.

The Californians swept past. I looked for my father, but I did not see him. Don Roberto raised his hand and waved to me. I still did not see my father. The lancers galloped hard for the lower part of the valley.

A second group of men rode out of the canyon. These were gringo soldiers, not officers. They charged toward the battlefield in the meadow where the officers sprawled in the grass. The soldiers saw our lancers fleeing westward down the valley. They raised their rifles and set off to pursue them.

They had not gone far when the lancers quickly wheeled, as they had done once before, and galloped back upon the soldiers. The soldiers, like the officers, now found that their rifles had rusted in the rain and would not shoot. They raised them to use as clubs, but our men struck hard with the long, deadly lances.

A horn sounded. More soldiers rode out of the canyon, and a wounded officer rallied them and retreated toward the hill that was covered with cactus. I could no longer see the lancers. I was now alone at the far side of the meadow.

The place where the battle was fought was strewn with soldiers. Some of them lay quiet in the grass and some cried for help. The battle had been brief. It had taken only a few minutes.

Lying dead before me there in the wet grass, I was soon to know, were almost twenty men of General Kearny's army, and as many wounded.

Not until much later, long after the battle of San Pasqual, did we learn about the gringo soldiers, where they had come from and what they had planned to do.

The blond gringo who had stopped at Dos Hermanos for food, Lieutenant Kit Carson, was with them. He was their guide and scout.

When Lieutenant Carson left Dos Hermanos, so we learned, and rode east with his message for President Polk, he met General Kearny a few leagues west of Santa Fe in New Mexico. He told the general that the war in California was over; the Spaniards hadn't fought and wouldn't fight and were a "passle of old women."

General Kearny partly believed Kit Carson and sent two thirds of his troops back to Santa Fe. He had orders to ride out to California and subdue the Spaniards, so he set out with one hundred and ten men for San Diego. He took Kit Carson with him, though Carson wanted to see his wife in Taos and take his message to President Polk.

They had traveled along the Devil's Highway and climbed the high mountains toward Agua Caliente. The men became exhausted, and most of the mules and horses sickened and died. At Agua Caliente, General Kearny had rested his men and caught more horses and started down the mountain for San Diego. It was there that our paths had joined.

These things we heard much later, after the bloody battle of San Pasqual had long been over.

← · **18** · →

A soldier got up from the place where his comrades lay and came toward the clump of oak trees where the horses were hidden. I don't think he saw me. He came slowly, dragging a rifle behind him.

I still did not see the lancers. The gringos were far across the meadow. They seemed to be getting ready to climb the hill that was covered with cactus. I watched the soldier coming toward me. He had lost his hat and there was a gash on his forehead.

The soldier didn't see me until he was standing under the first of the oak trees, looking at the horses. He was trying to decide which horse to take.

He stood glancing around. He must have felt that someone was there because when he saw me sitting on my horse under the oak, he didn't act surprised. He lifted the rifle he had been dragging and held it in both hands.

He cleared his throat and said, "Get down." He spoke Spanish, but poorly.

I held tight to the lance with its tip of Toledo
steel. I had no other weapon except a small blade
strapped to my leg. I could not use the lance if I
dismounted, for it needed not only a thrust but
the speed of my horse behind it.

"Get down," the gringo said once more.

He backed off two long steps and raised the
rifle. We looked at each other. He had a thin
mouth and a snubbed nose and hard blue eyes.

I wheeled Tiburón. I crouched low behind his
shoulder and swung behind the nearest tree.
Then, as the rifle exploded, a shot tore into the
branches over my head. I set the spurs and the
lance.

Tiburón bolted forward. The lance struck the
gringo in the shoulder and he fell backward
against the trunk of a tree and lay still. I got off
my horse. The gringo was breathing. The gash on
his forehead no longer bled.

All the gringos had left the meadow and were
climbing the hill, but our lancers were nowhere to
be seen. I was alone with a wounded man. There
were many others who were wounded lying in the
meadow.

The young soldier was tall but he was not
heavy. Still, I could not hope to lift him onto a
horse or hold him there if I did. I stood looking
down at him. His eyes were closed. He looked

very young, as if he should be home somewhere and not lying wounded here, in a strange meadow.

A cannon went off from beyond the meadow, in the direction of the hill that was covered with cactus. Another shot was fired. The sound of moaning came from the meadow as the sun rose and the mist burned off. My horses grew impatient.

When Don César Peralta rode up, I was still standing there by the wounded gringo, unable to decide what it was best to do.

Don César glanced at the soldier. "One more," he said, and looked at me for a moment. "There is good news and news that is not good. Your father was knocked from his horse. The horse was killed. Another is needed."

We selected the biggest of the seven horses and I put my saddle on him and we crossed the meadow to a wooded *barranca,* where my father lay. He was not able to stand or talk and his eyes were closed. Four of the men lifted him to the gelding's back and we took him out of the draw. We went back to the clump of oak trees. The gringo had not moved.

"We will make a travois," Don César said, and he sent two of the vaqueros off to cut strong saplings. "Don Saturnino cannot stay here in the open. Dos Hermanos is close."

The vaqueros made a travois of sapling boughs and two ponchos stretched over the frame. With riatas they made a makeshift harness and fastened the travois to the saddle on one of the horses.

"You can ride the gelding as far as the river," Don César said. "I will send some of your vaqueros ahead to Dos Hermanos and have them return to the river in an ox cart, which can be used for the rest of the journey. The fighting is over. We will keep the gringos on the hill for a night or two, but we cannot keep them there any longer. We have won the battle, not the war. But we have shown them that we are not old women, which is a thing of importance."

While they were placing my father on the travois, I went over to where the soldier lay. His eyes were closed but he was still breathing. The lance wound in his shoulder bled slowly.

I went back and spoke to Don César. "I will take the gringo also," I said.

He was surprised. "Take him where?"

"To Dos Hermanos."

"For what reason?"

"Because he is wounded and may die."

Don César pointed to the meadow. "There are

109

many there who are already dead and others who will die. We will take him there and leave him for the gringos. They will appear at nightfall, in the darkness."

I looked at Don César. "I take the soldier also," I said. "I take him to Dos Hermanos."

"Santa María," Don César said. He shook his head and muttered a curse under his breath that I was not meant to hear. But he went with the vaqueros and helped them to lay the gringo on the travois.

A cold wind was blowing when we started for the river. Three vaqueros went with me. One I sent ahead to carry the news to Dos Hermanos. My father did not know that he lay on the travois close beside the young soldier.

We came to the river at nightfall. Juan, the vaquero I had sent ahead, had reached Dos Hermanos and had returned to meet us. He brought
with him two litters, as well as horses and vaqueros.

The water was shallow, so we crossed the San
Luis without trouble. There was no moon, but we
knew the trail. Before midnight we were on the
open mesa and Dos Hermanos lay in front of us.

Pine torches burned along the walls. The big
gate was open; servants were running everywhere; the eagle was screaming. My grandmother
stood in the courtyard, where more torches
burned. As the two litters were carried through
the gate, she looked at me and said fiercely, "This
is your fault. Without you, Don Saturnino would
not have ridden off to fight an army. A foolhardy
act, and one you did not discourage."

I did not answer, knowing that words were of
little use. But I wondered if she were not right,
that if in some way the fault could be mine.

Don Saturnino and the soldier lay quietly on

the pine-bough litters. The soldier had said a word or two from time to time that I did not understand. Don Saturnino had lain with his eyes closed, without speaking. It was hard for him to breathe. He had a deep wound in his chest.

We carried him into the big *sala* and laid him upon his bed. The gringo we put in a room at the opposite side of the patio, as far from my father as we could. Doña Dolores had already sent off a vaquero to bring back help. There was only one surgeon in the pueblo and none in the country between.

When the surgeon came the next evening at dusk, he looked after the soldier first since he was a gringo. The gash the soldier had received in the battle was not serious, but he had lost blood from the lance wound.

"He is young," the surgeon said. "And the young don't die easily. That's why they do well in the army."

My father had been struck by a bullet during the first skirmish in the meadow. The bullet had entered his chest and gone out his back.

"Your father may live. He also may die," the surgeon told me and my grandmother and Yris, who had come from the Peralta ranch. "It is serious."

He showed the servants what to do for my

father and left salve and a jar of medicine. He wanted a good saddle horse in payment. Instead, we gave him two horses.

"If Don Saturnino worsens," he said as he made ready to ride away, "send word and I will come."

"When does the gringo leave?" Doña Dolores said.

"In another week," the surgeon said.

"Before?"

"No, señora."

"Since he has come this far," Doña Dolores said, "why can he not travel farther, perhaps to the pueblo?"

"He is not to be moved," the surgeon said. "He rests here for a week."

He climbed on his horse, and the Indian boy who had come with him got on one of the two mares we had given in payment.

"Mind you, señora," the surgeon said, "the young man is a soldier in the American Army. Be careful to treat him with respect. Remember that the gringos are now in charge."

"With respect?" my grandmother said, as the surgeon and the Indian boy rode away. "He will be treated well, with courtesy. That is all."

The soldier's name was John F. Fleming. I don't know what the F in his name stood for and I didn't ask him. He had lived in the Spanish town of Santa Fe for three months and during that time he had gained a little of the language.

The third day he was with us I took him a cup of chocolate, which he liked. I stood in the doorway before saying good night. A candle was burning by his bed. He had a thin face and the candlelight made it seem thinner than when I saw him first, with a rifle in his hand, coming toward me out of the meadow.

"I could have killed you," he said.

"You tried," I said. "You came close."

"I fired to scare you. And only when I saw you were not a man. I was a little surprised when my rifle went off. It was one of the few rifles in the company that didn't rust in the rain. But I always took good care of my rifles. My father taught me to."

"How was I to know that you were shooting just to scare me?"

"You should know that I meant no harm."

"Then what was the rifle for?"

"It belonged to me," the soldier said, speaking Spanish, "and I was carrying it. What was I supposed to do? Leave it behind in the meadow?"

"Why did you bring the rifle here to California?"

He raised up in bed a little and made a painful face. "I am a soldier in the army and when I am

told to march, I must march. With my rifle, natu-
rally."

"But why did you march here from a far place
to use the rifle on us?"

He looked at me as if I were crazy.

"What did we do?" I said. "What harm have we
done to make you wish to kill us?"

"Kill you? Who said anything about killing you?
We heard that there was still some fighting going
on, so we came out here to stop it."

He finished his drink and muttered a few words
of thanks. "You make good chocolate here, better
than they do at home," he said. "I like California,
what I've seen of it. It was pretty, leaving the
desert and coming up the mountain through the
pine trees, finding hot springs flowing right out of
the ground."

He looked around the room. At the white walls
and the beams and the floor that was made of ox
blood mixed with earth, worn smooth and shiny
by many feet.

"The ranchos are big in California," he said.
"Big as some states in the United States. Some
have sixty thousand acres, I hear. How many do
you own here on this rancho?"

"Many," I said.

"What is the name of your rancho?"

"El Rancho de los Dos Hermanos."

"Pretty name," the soldier said. "How many sisters do you have, señorita? I have three. They are ten, twelve, thirteen."

"Only one."

"Is she married?"

"Yes."

"Do you have brothers?"

"One, but he is dead."

The soldier poured himself a spoonful of the medicine the surgeon had left. "I never thought to be among such pretty señoritas," he said.

"You are not among them," I said.

I closed the door behind me and went along the *portale* to my room. The night was calm but the big eagle was restless on his perch.

‹ 20 ·›

As I came in the next morning Don Saturnino opened his eyes and stared at the wooden crucifix above the doorway. *"Dónde estoy?"* he said. These were his first words since the day of the battle at San Pasqual, at least that I had heard.

"You are home," I said, answering his question. "In your bed at Dos Hermanos."

He looked at the sunlight on the windowsill. The eagle screamed in the courtyard and he listened until it was silent. "At home," he said. "It is as you say. Everything is here. But why, where have I been?"

"You were wounded in the battle and we brought you home."

"The battle, yes, that I now remember. How did we fare against the gringo? My comrades, how are they?"

"The battle is won. The gringos have fled. Your friends are safe."

"No one dead, no one injured?"

"Only you, Don Saturnino."

"Everyone was brave, including Don Roberto?"

117

"Especially Don Roberto," I said.

The talk was tiring him, so I fixed the pillows under his head, gave him a drink of cold water, and slipped away. Don Saturnino had survived. I went to our chapel and knelt down in the candlelight, the warm lights that always burned there, and prayed. I gave thanks that my father was better and that with help he would now live.

I left the chapel and went out into the windy dawn with the faith that my prayers would be answered. And it seemed for a time that they would be answered.

The next morning Don César Peralta rode up with two of his vaqueros. He made a great commotion until the big gate was swung open. Then he rode through into the courtyard and tethered his horse — he was the only person my father permitted to ride his horse through the gate — and began shouting.

"*Hola*, Don Saturnino. Where do you hide? Under the bed? Come out, the battle is over." He strutted around the courtyard, jangling his spurs, taking his sombrero off and putting it back. "Come, *amigo*, we will protect you."

I told him how sick my father had been.

"We will cheer him up," said Don César.

And he did, almost at once. The two men no sooner had embraced than he began to recount all the things that had happened during the last days at San Pasqual.

"We drove the gringos out of the meadow," Don César said. "We scattered them like rabbits. Then they left the field and retreated up the hill, the one that is covered with cactus."

"How many of the rabbits did we kill?" my father asked.

"Two dozen, more or less. And many wounded. They dragged their wounded up the hill and we allowed them to do so. Somehow they got their rifles and cannon to work. Therefore we remained out of range and contented ourselves with riding around the hill, hurling insults."

"No more?"

"Much more. *Mucho más*," Don César said, pausing to ask me for a small bite to eat. Since I wanted to hear what happened, I sent a servant to bring a bowl of frijoles and a handful of tortillas.

"The gringos stayed on the hill all night. At dawn they put their wounded on travois and retreated down the valley to a peak, which they climbed. They camped then on the peak that night."

"No fighting?" my father asked.

"None," Don César said. "But the peak, we knew, was without water, and the gringos had no

119

food. They ate some of their mules to relieve their hunger. And, though I was against it, my son Roberto insisted upon hoisting a white flag and sending them sugar and tea."

"*Sancta Trinidad*, sugar and tea?"

"Sometimes my son has a soft head."

"That he inherits," my father said, with his first smile in many days.

"We kept up a heavy patrol, thinking to starve the gringos out. But that night in the darkness El Lobo escaped."

"El Lobo?"

"That is what he is called. It is the name he was called when he was here in California months ago. His name is Carson, Christopher Carson, and he is a scout for this big Army of the West."

"Army of the West?" my father said.

"That is what they call themselves."

"We defeated an army? We scattered it like rabbits?"

"Like rabbits," said Don César.

"But about the escape of El Lobo?"

"Yes, about him. We had a heavy patrol around the peak that night, as I have said, but somehow El Lobo got through. The next morning we found his boots in the chaparral so he must have taken them off."

"He took the boots off so as to go quietly?"

"That is true."

"El Lobo is a good name for such a man. What else did this wolf do?"

"He walked twenty leagues on feet without boots to the pueblo of San Diego, where there are some gringo soldiers and some war vessels."

"Then you left the peak to the gringos?" my father said.

"There was nothing else."

"But we won the battle."

"Yes, *amigo,* we won. We scattered the big gringo army like rabbits."

"Like rabbits," my father said. *"Como los conejos?"*

"Yes, like rabbits, Señor Don Saturnino."

← · **21** · →

The soldier grew stronger. He left his bed and went into the courtyard to sit in the sun and watch Rosario feed the big eagle. I could not keep him from leaving his room. But I was fearful that my father would hear him there or see him.

"Do you feel well enough to get on a horse?" I asked him on that morning, as he watched Rosario toss a mouse to Vuelo Grande.

"You want to get rid of me?" the gringo said.

"My father may wish to use the patio also," I said. "He likes the sun and he often feeds the eagle. He can do neither while you are here."

"Why? I'm not in his way. We can sit in the sun together and talk. We can talk about the battle, as old veterans should."

The young soldier was in a good mood, as if he were at home at Dos Hermanos.

"Don Saturnino is better, as I have told you, but he needs to walk and enjoy the sun. He does not know that you are here. He does not like gringos or gringo soldiers and you are both."

"You speak out," the young man said. "I have a sister like you. Whatever she thinks she says, no matter what."

"Can you go tomorrow?" I said. "If you're not able to ride a horse by then we will have a cart and a pair of oxen for you."

"I can go," the soldier said. He did not seem angry but I would not have blamed him if he had been.

Vuelo Grande, full of mice and gophers, was dozing with his eyes half-closed. He was a handsome bird. His black-banded tail, of which he was very proud and which he spent much time combing with his yellow beak, shone in the sun.

"I like that bird," Señor Fleming said. "He wouldn't be for sale, would he? I'd like to take him along to show my friends. I can tell them that he was sitting on a branch and I lassooed him."

The soldier reached out and gave the banded tail a friendly twist. More from rage than from injury the eagle flapped his wings and let out one of his loudest screams.

"The eagle belongs to my father," I said. "And he's not likely to sell him."

"I'll ask; won't do any harm," the soldier said. "He's standing over there now." The soldier raised his hand in a greeting. "*Hola,* señor," he called out.

123

My father did not answer. He came slowly across the courtyard. He looked pale.

"I was asking about your eagle," the soldier said. "Your daughter says you don't want to sell it."

I doubt that my father heard the soldier. He did not look at him. He looked at me for a long time. He was trying to control the wrathful words crowding into his throat.

"I have learned this morning from one of our vaqueros that you brought a gringo to Dos Hermanos," he said at last. "I did not believe this, but now I see that it is true."

"I'll explain," the soldier said.

My father did not answer him. He acted as if the gringo were not there, standing not two steps away.

"He leaves at once," Don Saturnino said. "I have given orders for a cart to take him away, to any place he wishes to go."

The soldier said, "I can tell you why I am here."

"I know why you are here," my father said, still not looking at the soldier. To me he said, "I will talk to you later about this." He was angry, close to silence. He was thinking of Carlos. Our eyes met.

Always before I had done what my father

124

wished, and I was always a loving and obedient daughter. What he wished me to do I had done, without so much as thinking about it. But as we stood there with him trying to stare me down, I remembered suddenly the moment in the meadow when I had used the lance and there was no other thought in my mind than to thrust it through the soldier's heart. I was ashamed, now, of what I had tried to do. The shame gave me courage. It is important to speak, I thought. Then I said, "This man has been wounded. I wounded him myself. The surgeon told me not to move him for a week and the week has not passed."

My father winced at these words. "It would be better had I died at San Pasqual," he said quietly, but as though he spoke the very truth. "Far better."

His face was white. He took a step toward the soldier and stopped, as if in pain. Thinking to help him, I put a hand on his arm but he pulled away. He parted his lips and wet them with his tongue. He tried to speak to me, to the soldier, to someone. Looking at the sky, he slowly sank to his knees. The soldier caught him and laid him in the sun on the beaten earth of the courtyard.

My father breathed for a while, deep breaths, as if he wanted to take in the whole world. I went to call my grandmother. When we returned, my father was breathing in great gasps. I called the Indians, and we took him to his bed. He did not speak again. Late that night, as we sat beside him, Don Saturnino de Zubarán turned his face toward us and, looking at us from far away, died.

◄ 22 ►

Father Barones came to the ranch two days later and we buried Don Saturnino in our chapel beside his father and his beloved son. Vaqueros played sad music on their violas. It was a windless day with bright skies. Friends came from all around, but they did not stay after the big dinner at noonday.

After they had gone, I went to see the gringo, who had not come to the funeral because he had not been invited. He was lying in bed, looking pale and forlorn.

"It's time for me to go," he said. "I'm not very strong, but I can't lie around here forever."

"I understand how you feel," I said, eager that he leave. "You can travel by oxcart or by horseback. I'll send vacqueros with you."

"I ought to go tomorrow," the soldier said, "if the weather holds good."

"I'll see that everything is ready."

"I ought to leave early in the morning. By horseback."

I saw that everything was ready for the soldier

at dawn — two good horses to ride and three vaqueros to look after him, and ample food for the two-day journey. But when Diaz, the *mayordomo*, went to call him, he was still in bed.

"He sleeps," the *mayordomo* reported.

"Arouse him," I said.

The *mayordomo* went off but came back in a few minutes.

"He still sleeps," *Mayordomo* Diaz said.

"Have you tried cold water?" I asked.

"Is that your wish?"

"It is my wish," I said, but as the *mayordomo* strode off toward the well to fill a bucket I relented. "Let him sleep for another hour."

We waited an hour, for two hours, for three. When he continued to sleep, the *mayordomo* shook him awake and reminded him that this was the day he was to leave for San Diego. The soldier asked for me and, out of sorts, I went trudging off to his room.

He was sitting up in bed, looking more forlorn than he had the day before.

"I feel weak," he said in a very weak voice.

"Then you do not wish to leave today?"

"Perhaps tomorrow," he said. "I should feel better in a day or two."

But on the morrow the soldier was still not ready to go, nor on the following day.

"Do you want me to send for the doctor?" I asked him.

"That will not be necessary," he said. "I feel a little stronger every day."

And he looked strong as he sat there in the bed, his blue eyes clear and alert. It struck me suddenly that he had chosen to be an invalid, that he was playing a game to delay leaving the ranch as long as he possibly could.

"If you are not better by tomorrow or the next day, I will send for the doctor," I told him.

The thought of my calling the doctor brought a shadow over his face.

"The doctor has a lot to do," he said. "I'd feel like an old woman, asking him to make a long journey out here just to look after me."

In two days he was back on his feet, and on the third day we sent him off with three vaqueros for the pueblo of San Diego.

"I hope there are no hard feelings," he said as he settled himself in the saddle.

"None," I answered. "May you go with God."

He blew me sort of a kiss, which embarrassed me in front of the vaqueros, and said, *"Hasta la vista,"* which means, roughly, in English words, "Until we meet." This embarrassed me also because I really did not wish to see him again.

23

We had no rain that winter. Wherever you dug, the earth was dry. A few showers came in April, but by June the grass and filaree had shriveled up and died. It was a bad year for us and many of our friends.

In June, on a day when white clouds were wandering around on the horizon, my grandmother and I sat in the parlor and talked about the drought.

"A year ago," Doña Dolores said, "we sat in this very *sala* and watched the rain pouring from the sky."

"And coming down through the roof," I reminded her.

"We caught it in jugs."

We both tried to laugh. Rosario, who crouched in front of Doña Dolores, tried to laugh also. She told him to shut his mouth, that this business of the drought was not funny.

Doña Dolores would have liked to blame me for the drought, but somehow she just couldn't make a connection between the weather and the way I ran things.

After my father's death the problems of the ranch fell upon my shoulders. I had learned about the workshops and I could ride with the vaqueros, but still I was not ready to run Dos Hermanos. I had looked to my father to make decisions since I was old enough to remember. Now the decisions were suddenly mine. I could not count upon Doña Dolores, upon anyone, only upon myself.

The worst trouble I had at this time came from the *mayordomo,* Juan Diaz. The first order I gave made him angry.

"Can you take some of the vaqueros," I said to him, "and dig a new well? The one in the patio is giving us a scarce ten gallons a day."

Diaz was part Indian, solid as a tree stump, a young man of many talents. I wanted to keep him, so I spoke softly and asked if he could undertake the task. He was not used to receiving orders or even suggestions from a woman, a sixteen-year-old at that.

"A new well," he replied, "will yield no more water than the old."

"Are you certain?" I asked.

"Yes."

"Why are you certain?"

This question puzzled him, but he said, "There

131

are things that you know and things that you do not know."

"True," I said. "And one of the things I know is that we need more water. Perhaps you would prefer to build a flume from the stream and bring it to the house that way?"

The stream was half a league away. Trees would have to be felled, sawn to length, fastened together with pitch and rawhide. It would be a difficult task and a long one.

"You can take your choice," I said, "but we must have water."

The *mayordomo* turned away, grumbling under his breath, but that afternoon he began a new well outside the walls in a nearby meadow. Two days later he sulkily announced that we had a new well. It yielded more water than the old one.

Juan Diaz never got used to taking orders from me but he did the work I gave him, as did the others: the blacksmiths, the leather-workers, the cooks, servants, and the vaqueros, the herdsmen who cared for the cattle and horses.

It was the vaqueros who were my friends and on whom I leaned and depended. It was these men who saw us through the worst drought in the memory of anyone then living.

The drought started early in the year, as I have

said, and by June the hills were bare. Cattle began to die. Waterholes dried up. The stream shrank and we had to dig holes in the stream bed to tap small quantities of the water that ran beneath it.

In July we began the slaughter. Because everyone, all the ranchers from San Diego in the South to Santa Barbara in the North, were forced to kill their cattle, hides sold for only a few centavos and there was no market for tallow at any price. We stored almost a thousand *botas* against the time when it would bring a few centavos at least. The hides we could not cure or store, so we buried them in pits.

We struggled on through the month of August. We were sad at the sight of our cattle and horses dying. September was the time our first rains usually came, but this year clouds blew up in the afternoon and then disappeared at dusk. We ourselves began to run low on food, not on beef, because our coolhouse was stacked with meat, but on tea and chocolate, flour, sugar, salt, and on beans, which the servants and the vaqueros ate, liking them better than anything else.

Around the middle of September I took four of the vaqueros and extra pack horses and made the long journey to San Diego. Before the drought it was easy to get credit, but I found that the pueblo store now belonged to a gringo. Worried by the drought, I was afraid to buy all the goods we needed. Not knowing when I could pay for them, we packed the horses with only light loads.

When the time came for me to pay for the supplies, I asked the storekeeper, whose name was Caleb Thomas, to charge them to Dos Hermanos.

Mr. Thomas was a thin little man with a friendly smile, gold spectacles, and a pale nose. "You are buying lightly," he said. "Looking at your past account, I would say that you have bought about half of what you usually buy."

"I don't know when we can pay even for what I have," I said.

"The drought will end one of these days," Mr. Thomas said. "Until then, your credit is good. Let me give you a jug of Jamaica molasses. It just came in today."

He led me over to a counter and showed me a length of blue cloth. "Just in from Boston. The newest material. And these shoes; fashionable New York ladies are wearing them."

Mr. Thomas hopped from counter to counter, showing me everything that had arrived that day by ship.

My heart sank as I signed the bill. It was for

more money than we usually spent on supplies for the ranch, even in good years. But I did have a big packet of Cuban tobacco for Doña Dolores and a beautiful China shawl for myself as well as a black bombazine dress that had real lace around the collar. As I rode away from the store and Mr. Thomas waved me goodbye, I felt very light-headed.

24

September passed and the drought grew worse.
Every day a dozen or more cattle died. The working horses we managed to feed by cutting
branches from the willow groves along the stream.
Our Indians caught rattlesnakes in the heavy
brush, carried them across the barren mesa at
dawn, and let them loose, telling them to beseech
the rain gods. Doña Dolores and I knelt at the
altar and prayed. But the rains did not come.

On a hot day early in December, Caleb Thomas
rode up to the ranch on a beautiful white gelding.
His saddle sparkled with silver and the metal
crickets on his bridle chirped as he trotted up to
the hitching rack.

"I'm sorry to see everything so dry," he said,
after he had taken my hand. "And hundreds of
cattle dying and the horses gaunt."

He stood for a while, gazing around at the mesa,
the tree-lined streams winding westward, the far
blue hills that slanted away toward the sea.

"How many acres do you have here?" he asked.
He had a chirpy voice. Any moment I expected

him to burst into song, like a bird. "Sixty thousand?"

"Less."

"Have you ever thought of selling part of it?"

"No."

"You have a parcel down by the coast, where the stream meets the ocean. Five hundred acres, more or less. I can make you a good offer."

The parcel he spoke about was near the lagoon where the wreck of the treasure ship lay.

"You will need to talk to my grandmother. But I can tell you now that she will not be interested in selling."

"At a good price?"

"At any price."

"Do you mind if I talk to her?"

I led Mr. Thomas into the patio and sent for Doña Dolores. She took her time but finally came stumping out of the *sala*, swinging her cane. I introduced them and told my grandmother that the Cuban tobacco she liked so much I had bought from Mr. Thomas.

"It is the best I have smoked since some Turkish that I bought from a New Bedford whaler."

"Had I known that you liked it so much," said Mr. Thomas, "I would have brought some along as a gift."

He was making a good impression upon my

grandmother, but it didn't last long.

"I spoke to Miss Carlota about a parcel of land on the coast," Mr. Thomas said. "Some five hundred acres of brush and water, mostly brush not fit for cattle. But I'm prepared to offer you twenty-five centavos an acre. The going price for such land is twenty, as you know."

"My land is worth ten times that," Grandmother said sharply.

"Before the drought, maybe," Mr. Thomas said. "Not now. Everything's dried up at this moment — range, pasture, meadows, hills, streams. And the Lord knows when it will be any better. Perhaps never."

Doña Dolores rolled a cigarillo and Rosario brought her a live coal. She puffed away and said nothing.

Mr. Thomas said, "What do you think, señora?"

"I am not thinking," my grandmother answered.

"I can offer you twenty-five centavos an acre," Caleb Thomas repeated.

"Two hundred centavos," said Doña Dolores, "and I will begin to think. Not much, but a little."

"Ridiculous," cried Mr. Thomas. "How about fifty?"

"Two hundred," Doña Dolores said firmly.

Mr. Thomas took off his spectacles and polished them on his sleeve.

"Fifty-five centavos."

Doña Dolores did not bother to answer. She turned to me and asked what we were having for supper, saying that she was becoming very tired of peppers and tough meat.

Mr. Thomas began to walk up and down in front of us, hopping like an angry bird. At last, when Doña Dolores went on talking as if he weren't there, he stopped and pulled a piece of paper from his jacket and held it out in front of my grandmother. He gave the paper a shake and then pointed at it with a long finger.

"Madam," he said, "what do you propose to do with this?"

Doña Dolores puffed on her cigarillo and glanced at the paper through the cigarillo smoke.

"What is it?" she asked.

"It's a bill for the goods and supplies your granddaughter bought some three months ago."

"Bills we pay once a year," Doña Dolores said. "On All Saints' Day."

"This bill," said Mr. Thomas, "must be paid immediately."

Doña Dolores planted her cane, leaned upon it, and lifted herself to her feet. "On All Saints' Day we pay our bills," she said.

Mr. Thomas folded the paper and put it back in his pocket. "Unless I hear from you by next week," he said, "I'll turn the bill over to the sheriff and attach your property."

"I will speak to the *juez de campo*," Doña Dolores said. She raised her cane as if she had a mind to strike him over the head. "He will attend to you."

"*Juez de campo*," said Mr. Thomas with a trace of pity in his voice. "Is it possible, señora, that you have not heard that Americans are now in charge of California? That the *juez de campo* has long since departed? Is it possible, I inquire?"

My grandmother tossed her cigarillo on the ground, crushed it out with the tip of her cane, and stumped off to the *sala*, slamming the door behind her.

Mr. Thomas looked startled for a moment, as he settled his long gray riding coat around his shoulders. He reminded me of a little gray sparrow ruffling its feathers. He coughed and took the paper from his pocket and held it under my nose.

"You bought these things, did you not?" he said in a pleasant voice.

"Yes," I answered.

"And you intend to pay for them?"

"Yes."

"Good," Mr. Thomas said. "Bring the money to the store when you come again."

He smiled and got on his horse and tipped his hat.

But as he rode away a sudden suspicion took hold of me. I doubted that he would wait for the money we owed. I had no idea what the American law was, but what if he took the bill straight to the American authorities, whoever they were, and somehow got the right to seize our property? I became certain of it as he paused for a moment on the rim of the mesa and gazed around at the rolling hills of Dos Hermanos.

The next morning I took two extra horses and Rosario and rode down the canyon to the lagoon where the wreck of the galleon lay.

The stream was low but the tides had piled up many logs and heaps of seaweed around the cavelike hole I used to reach the ship. It took us until noon to clear away the debris.

As I tied the riata around Rosario's waist, I remembered the day when I had nearly drowned in the jaws of the burro clam. And I remembered it as I let myself down into the hole. The water was cold and murky. I kept the end of the riata wrapped around my hand. I had told Rosario to keep tight hold of the other end and his mind on what he was doing.

Everything looked the same — the thick layers

of silt, the big rocks, the floating strands of sea-weed, the chest. Nearby stood the gray burro clam, its jaws half-open to embrace anything that strayed near. A film of river mud concealed the gold coins. When I had scraped it off, my lungs were hurting and it was time for me to go above. A small shark followed me.

The sun was overhead but it gave off little heat. I stood on the riverbank and swung my arms, trying to get warm, but I was really trying to get up my nerve to go back again. Rosario wasn't interested in the coins but he wanted to explore the wreck. I had a good notion to let him.

A shark trailed me down, floating off as I raised the hand that held my knife, but turning just out of reach to watch me. I could see its gills opening and closing. It was only half my size but it had mean little eyes set close together and flecked with red, and three rows of teeth, one row set back of the other.

Small fish were swimming around the chest. They darted away as I pried the first handful of coins loose. I put the coins in the sack that was tied to my waist, carried them up, and laid them out on a log.

On the third trip below, I reached the bottom of the chest and saw that it was now empty. I put the coins in the pouch, stepped wide of the burro clam, and made my way up for the last time. I was very glad that it would be the last time.

We rubbed the coins bright, using the river sand, and took them back to the ranch. In the morning I set off for San Diego and traded the coins for American dollars, enough to pay Mr. Thomas, with a bagful to spare.

Mr. Thomas, I am sure, was disappointed that I was able to pay my bill but he didn't let on. He smiled and patted my arm, and tried to sell me a coat with a band of otter fur on the collar.

◄ · 25 · ►

Rains came with the New Year and they lasted for more than a month. We had managed to save half our cattle, all of our working horses, and some of the *mesteños*. But most of these wild horses in our part of the country Don Roberto had rounded up, because there wasn't food for them, and had driven over the high cliffs at Punta de Laguna.

When the spring grass was just beginning to show, Mr. Thomas rode up to the ranch and announced that he had come for beef cattle. He bought seventy tough steers, paying us ninety centavos a head, and drove them off the same day to San Diego. About a month later I found out why he had bought the cattle. Juan Diaz, our *mayordomo*, came back from San Diego with a wild tale.

"Early in the morning," the *mayordomo* told us, "that was three months ago in January, a man named Marshall, who was a carpenter, was building a grist mill for a man named Sutter. He had just finished building a flume from the river to the mill. One morning he went down to the flume to shut off the water. There at the bottom of the flume he saw a piece of what he thought might be gold. He pounded it between rocks and when it changed its shape but did not break in two he was certain it was gold. Almost certain, that is.

"A few days later he went to Sutter's and showed him the pieces he had found in the flume. They tested them and proved they were gold. Right then the two men decided to keep what they found a big secret. But shortly afterward a man named Brannon found some gold and he galloped to San Francisco and rode down the streets, shaking a bottle of gold dust over his head and shouting, 'Gold! Gold! Gold from the American River.'

"Within a week all the sailors in San Francisco harbor deserted their ships. Carpenters dropped their hammers. A nearby town opened its jail. Thousands flocked to the mill and clawed it to pieces, looking for gold. Three Frenchmen pulled up a tree stump and found a fortune in gold hanging on to its roots. Imagine, if you are able, a fortune from a tree stump."

Two days after he had told us this tale, Juan Diaz took six horses from our corral and rode off at a gallop for the North.

We all thought Juan was crazy but he was not crazy. The story he told us was true. Before the month of May was gone, a steady line of men on horses began to troop up the King's Highway, along the western boundary of Dos Hermanos. They were on their way to the gold fields.

When I went to San Diego, I learned that these men, about four hundred of them, had crossed the Isthmus of Panama and there bought passage to San Francisco. But the crooked captain of the ship carried them only as far as San Diego. He told them they were in San Francisco, and then sailed back to Panama to pick up another cargo, leaving the men stranded two hundred leagues south of the gold fields.

Our vaqueros reported that the gold-seekers stole a band of horses and slaughtered our cows during the first few days, so I went down to the Highway to move our stock out of reach.

A herd of cattle had strayed, and these we drove back. I had three vaqueros with me. As we crossed the Highway we encountered two men riding white geldings and leading two mares. I knew the horse by sight; they bore the Z brand of Dos Hermanos. As we pulled up in front of them, I thought of the time my father and I had stopped the band of gringo thieves.

"The geldings belong to Dos Hermanos," I said to the two young men.

I was still angry that we had found the carcasses

of more than forty cows scattered along the King's Highway. The gringos at least could have slaughtered our steers and not our breeding stock. I spoke in Spanish. The one with the long blond hair and blue eyes looked puzzled. The other young man answered me in Spanish and I saw that he *was* a Spaniard.

"We bought the horses," he said.

"That story I am acquainted with," I said. "I have heard it many times and I am tired of hearing it."

"I repeat, señorita. The horses we have bought. We paid ten pesos apiece for them. Except one of the mares, which cost four pesos."

He turned away and spoke to the gringo in the gringo language. Whereupon the young man with the long blond hair fumbled around in a small bag he had tied to his saddle horn and pulled out a piece of paper. He swung his horse around, edged up to me, and handed it over. At the top of the paper were the words "Sunrise Grocery Store" and, below it, "Caleb Thomas, Prop." Farther down was a notation, and then a signature that I recognized as belonging to Thomas.

"Mr. Thomas," I said, "did not own the horses he sold you. They bear our brand."

The Spaniard spoke to the gringo, who continued to look puzzled. I noticed a name in gilt

147

letters on the valise he had tied to his saddle. It read "Dr. John Brett."

The gringo fumbled around again in his valise and pulled out some paper money, a fistful, and handed it to me. "*Perdón*," he said.

The Spaniard said, "He wants to pay for the horses."

I looked at the gringo, who was not much older than I. I glanced at his long blond hair and blue eyes and the way his long legs hung down out of the stirrups. I glanced at his valise, which was very new, and at the fresh gilt letters that spelled out his name. He was the nicest-looking gringo I had seen.

"With your permission, the doctor and I will continue the journey," the Spaniard said. "I have a long way to go."

"Where are you bound?" I said, though I knew.

"To seek fortune in the gold field."

"And the other?" I said, pointing.

"He is a doctor and will pursue his profession somewhere along our coast. Perhaps in Santa Barbara."

"Tell your friend," I said, "that there are no doctors in the pueblo of San Diego or the country around. And only one that I know of in pueblo Los Angeles."

"I will impart your information," said the

Spaniard, who was one to talk importantly.

"Do not forget," I reminded him.

The white gelding the young doctor was riding had a bad way, I remembered, of shying at anything that moved suddenly — a twig, a bush, anything. I told one of the vaqueros to untie a gelding that we had with us. It was one of our best horses.

"Inform the doctor that the gelding he rides is not trustworthy. And ask him to dismount while my vaquero changes saddles."

The doctor got off his horse and stood holding his new valise. He looked much better standing on the ground than he did sitting in the saddle. When the new horse was saddled, he climbed up and tied his valise to the horn.

He said something in Spanish as they rode off along the King's Highway. He had a gringo's voice, but it was soft. I watched him bouncing up and down in the saddle, the small valise swinging from the saddle horn. I watched as he came to a little rise and then disappeared in the yellow dust and the bright sun.

◄· 26 ·►

My grandmother wanted to know what I had seen on my journey to the King's Highway. She was sitting in her *sala,* smoking Caleb Thomas's tobacco. Rosario stood nearby, waving a fan made of a manzanita branch.

"I found the carcasses of many cows," I said.

"The gringos?" Doña Dolores said.

"Yes."

"They are a swarm of insects."

"Not all," I said. "I encountered a doctor on the King's Highway. Señor Thomas had sold him some of our horses, and when I accused the doctor of stealing them he offered me a handful of money."

"Did you take it?"

"Yes," I answered. I decided to say nothing about giving the young gringo one of our best horses.

Doña Dolores said, "Horses and cattle should bring a price now that the gringos are upon us like insects. But what we need is someone to bargain with them. A man."

150

"I'll bargain."

"You would give the ranch away before the summer is out. A strong man should be in charge of Dos Hermanos, not a girl."

I said nothing more because I was too angry to trust my tongue.

Doña Dolores was watching me. "I do not mean to offend you," she said. "But I must speak the truth. The ranch is big. It has forty-seven thousand acres, all of them good. It is not a plaything. It requires strong hands. A man!"

I did not reply, but asked her permission to be away for a moment.

I went to the room where our leather goods were made. Here I picked up a footstool that had been lying around for a year and took it back to the *sala* and placed it on the floor in front of Doña Dolores.

"What is this?" she asked, eyeing the stool.

"A place for your feet."

"I have a place for my feet."

"Two more of our Indians have gone north to find gold," I said. "Rosario is needed."

My grandmother was smoking. She tossed the half-finished cigarillo in the fireplace and straightened herself. "He is needed here," she said, raising her voice. "Now and tomorrow. Here!"

The golden eagle was still screaming in the courtyard.

"Rosario is needed in other places," I said and, again asking my grandmother's permission, I left her to fume.

The big eagle was still screaming and Rosario was getting ready to feed him. It had always made me sad to see the great-winged bird sitting there in the courtyard, chained to a perch. Most of the time he sat with his feathers ruffled and his eyes half-closed.

I said to Rosario, "Let the eagle go."

"How? He has a chain."

"With a file, which you can borrow from the blacksmith, and use to file the chain."

"Would it not be better if the blacksmith filed the chain?"

"I wish you to file the chain."

"I leave," said Rosario.

When he came back we both used the file and cut the silver chain. The eagle did not know that he was free. He stood as he had stood before, drooping his wings, watching us with his golden eyes. I gave him a push and he fell on the ground. I pushed him again, which he answered with a claw. He craned his neck and walked away. He spread his wings and ever so softly rose above the gate and the roof. He made a circle above us and another still higher. Then he flew off toward the mountains, toward the high mesas beyond the mountains.

"He returns to the country he came from," I said.

"The Piute country," Rosario said.

"Do you wish to follow him?" I said.

"Yes. But how?"

"On a horse."

"What horse do you speak of?"

"A horse that I will give you."

"On Tiburón?"

The Piutes are not bashful Indians.

"No."

"On Sixto, señorita?"

"Sixto."

"And a saddle?"

"Yes."

"With silver?"

"With silver."

"A red poncho?"

"Red."

"When?"

"Now," I said, "because I have much work to do."